BRAIN STORM

Tap Into Your Creativity to Generate
Awesome Ideas and Remarkable Results

JASON R. RICH

CAREER
PRESS
Franklin Lakes, NJ

BRAIN STORM
EDITED BY CLAYTON W. LEADBETTER
TYPESET BY EILEEN DOW MUNSON
Cover design by Johnson Design
Printed in the U.S.A. by Book-mart Press

To order this title, please call toll-free 1-800-CAREER-1 (NJ and Canada: 201-848-0310) to order using VISA or MasterCard, or for further information on books from Career Press.

**ℬ CAREER
   PRESS**

The Career Press, Inc., 3 Tice Road, PO Box 687,
Franklin Lakes, NJ 07417
www.careerpress.com
Library of Congress Cataloging-in-Publication Data

Rich, Jason.
   Brain storm : tap into your creativity to generate awesome ideas and remarkable results / by Jason R. Rich.
      p. cm.
   Includes index.
   ISBN 1-56414-668-5 (pbk.)
      1. Creative ability in business. 2. Brainstorming. 3. Creative thinking. 4. Success in business. I. Title.

HD53 .R529 2003
650.1—dc21   2002191191

Acknowledgments

One of the keys to success in life is to surround yourself with smart, creative, and caring people you love and who provide endless support. Mark, Ellen, and Ferras (whom you'll be meeting later in this book), are the closest and dearest friends anyone could ever hope for. For their friendship, I am truly grateful. I'd also like to express my love and gratitude to my family, and dedicate this book to Emily.

In terms of this book, thanks to everyone who agreed to be interviewed and who so generously shared their time and experience. The people whose interviews you'll soon be reading will inspire anyone interested in learning to tap into their creativity.

I'd also like to thank Mike Lewis, Kirsten Beucler, Clayton Leadbetter, Eileen Munson, Briana Rosen, and everyone else at The Career Press, for helping to make *Brain Storm* a reality and for inviting me to work on this exciting project.

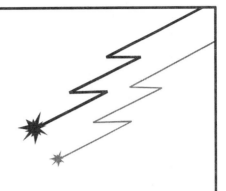

Contents

Preface

Creativity is allowing yourself to make mistakes. Art is knowing which ones to keep.

—Scott Adams

The world is filled with great ideas and with people who come up with them. Every new innovation, discovery, work of art, musical composition, novel, or business plan, for example, is sparked by someone's ideas. The power to think and generate incredible ideas lies within anyone who chooses to harness their own creative juices, tap into their creativity, and believe in the amazing powers of their own ideas.

Do you have what it takes to generate ideas that will ultimately lead to tremendous success in whatever it is you set out to achieve? The answer is an unequivocal yes! However, just as you have learned other skills, such as how to read, write, and do math, it is necessary to train yourself to properly harness the power of your brain in order to think creatively, brainstorm, and utilize your creativity.

No matter what you do for a living or where your personal interests lie, you can become more successful and achieve greater things if you're willing to "pop the top" on your brain and learn how to think more creatively as you confront life's trials and tribulations. Once you begin to discover how to generate incredible ideas, your true success will come from learning how to transform those ideas into reality.

Without exception, everyone can benefit from discovering the secrets of how to generate awesome ideas and then bring their best ideas into fruition. *Brain Storm: Tap Into Your Creativity to Generate Awesome Ideas and Remarkable Results* is your personal roadmap to better understanding the creative thinking and brainstorming process so you, too, can begin generating ideas with the power to change the world around you for the better.

Once you have learned the basics of how to generate ideas, evaluate, then implement the best of them, you will have a chance to learn directly from people who have already achieved incredible success as a direct result of their ability to think creatively, brainstorm, and generate incredible ideas.

The people interviewed in the later portion of this book include business professionals, entrepreneurs, artists, and entertainers, who have all discovered ways to achieve success in whatever they do by taping into their creativity.

Within a short time, you too will be generating new ideas, building upon other people's ideas, using your brain to find creative solutions to problems and challenges, and coming up with ideas that will improve your personal, professional, and financial life. Everyone has the ability to think, brainstorm, create, and innovate. What's holding you back from utilizing your creativity? For most people, it's fear or perhaps a lack of knowledge, skill, drive, and confidence to transform an idea into reality.

You Too Can Benefit From This Book

Don't think. Thinking is the enemy of creativity. It's self-conscious, and anything self-conscious is lousy. You can't try to do things. You simply must do things.

—Ray Bradbury

Everyone can benefit from mastering their ability to brainstorm new ideas and implement the best of their ideas into their personal and professional lives. The ability to generate incredible ideas has nothing to do with how smart you are.

Learning how to utilize this ability is what will ultimately help you achieve success in every aspect of your life. We all have challenges we face, obstacles to overcome, and goals we'd like to achieve. By properly using your creative thinking abilities, you will find innovative ways to take advantage of opportunities, plus you'll discover ways to develop new or alternative solutions to whatever problems, challenges, and obstacles you encounter. You'll ultimately be able to develop well-thought-out action plans for achieving your goals and dreams.

Everyone has heard the phrase "think outside the box," but what does it really mean? From this book, you will learn how to think differently and approach everyday situations in your life from a different perspective. You will discover why it is important to face problems, not with negative emotions or fear, but with the power of creativity.

Some people, including artists, writers, musicians, actors, scientists, and inventors, rely everyday on their creative abilities, yet even the most successful of these people sometimes hit creative road blocks. If your career depends on your creativity, or your life would somehow benefit from learning how to think and brainstorm more creatively, this book will help you.

As you overcome your fear of expressing your creativity, learn how to think like an innovator, and discover the secrets of awesome brainstorming, it's vital that you practice utilizing these new skills in order to master them. Just like any other skill, creative thinking and brainstorming skills need to be nurtured and perfected over time. This will take an investment of time, energy, and effort on your part, but the positive results will be dramatic.

> *An invasion of armies can be resisted, but not an idea whose time has come.*
>
> —Victor Hugo

How you decide to incorporate creative thinking into your life is up to you. The possibilities are truly limitless. As you begin to tap into your creative energies and achieve success, please share your experiences by e-mailing them to me at jr7777@aol.com. Who knows—maybe you'll find yourself being interviewed for a future edition of this book!

—Jason R. Rich
www.JasonRich.com

CHAPTER 1

The Next Big Idea Is Within You: Fundamentals of Brainstorming

At The Walt Disney World Resort in Orlando, Florida, one of the first attractions to open at Epcot Center was called "Journey Into Imagination." While on the surface, it might seem like this attraction is just for kids—because it features an adorable purple creature named "Figment" (as in *figment of your imagination*)—this attraction lightheartedly showcases how people, just like you and me, can use our imaginations and be creative and innovative thinkers. While this attraction has been revamped several times during the past decade, to millions of tourists, it continues to demonstrate just what it takes to use one's imagination.

From this attraction, adults can learn an important lesson: You're never too old to be creative, use your imagination, and become an innovative thinker—no matter what you're doing. While there are no cute songs or purple creatures flying around in the corporate world, chances are, you've heard catch phrases like, "think outside the box" or "think different." Companies of all sizes have begun to realize that creative thinkers can be a tremendous asset to an organization.

In fact, some of the largest and most influential corporations in the world have hired high-priced consultants for the sole purpose of helping senior level personnel to become more creative in the ways they conduct business.

Everyone (yes, you too) has an imagination, as well as the ability to think and be creative. The problem is, as most of us have grown up from childhood (when playing "make-believe" was a readily accepted pastime), we've been encouraged to leave our creativity behind and to think analytically. As adults, we overanalyze problems, learn to accept things as they are, follow the directions given by superiors, and become fearful of being criticized for having new and original thoughts that don't fit into the everyday norm.

During a business meeting, for example, too many people are afraid to voice their new ideas and opinions, or even go through the effort of generating those thoughts, simply because they're afraid of being shot down, not fitting in, or not being looked upon favorably by coworkers or superiors. If you've grown up and forgotten how to use your imagination and think creatively, you're about to take a dip in the fountain of youth and relearn some valuable skills!

Some adults, especially actors, artists, musicians, writers, inventors, and entrepreneurs, for example, have refused to totally abandon their creativity or stop using their minds to come up with new and innovative ideas. While these people might have given away their crayons, finger paints, and dress-up costumes from childhood, they have discovered that using their minds and looking at things differently can lead to incredible success. To be a creative thinker or expert brainstormer, however, you don't need to be an "artsy" person.

No matter who you are, or what you do for a living, *Brain Storm* is all about helping you to use your mind a little differently in order to be more creative and innovative. Creative thinking and the ability to brainstorm new ideas is a skill, much like reading, solving math problems, or using the computer. It's a skill that people already have, but don't necessarily know how to use properly. It's also a skill that takes time to nurture and develop before it can be truly mastered.

As you'll soon discover, creative thinking and brainstorming is all about generating new and innovative ideas for solving problems, addressing issues, or improving upon already existing ideas. Thus, no matter what types of issues you face in your professional, personal, or financial life, chances are, if you develop different perspectives for looking at things, you could improve upon a situation dramatically.

The ideas you need in order to improve your situation at work or at home, or that relate to your wallet, are all within your head—perhaps locked away, just waiting to be released. Good ideas, and most likely awesome ideas, are within you and this book will show you how to generate, analyze, and implement them.

In this chapter, we'll begin to explore what an idea actually is. There are many types of ideas and many reasons for generating them. Later, you'll learn how to brainstorm awesome ideas that generate tremendous results, then discover how to perfect your brainstorming skills and ultimately implement your ideas into your professional, personal, or financial life.

What Is an Idea, Anyway?

When you think about coming up with a great idea, perhaps you think of an imaginary light bulb lighting up above your head, as an expression that communicates, "Eureka! I've got it!" spreads across your face. Ideas are things your brain comes up with—sometimes when you want or need it to, and sometimes when you least expect it.

One definition of an idea, according to *The Merriam-Webster Dictionary,* is that it's a "formulated thought or opinion." Hey, you have thoughts and opinions, right? Perhaps this whole creativity and brainstorming concept won't be so difficult to learn after all. Who knows? It might even be fun!

Everyone has ideas. Around noon, perhaps you experience hunger, and you think to yourself, "Hmm, I want something to eat." The concept of getting something to eat is an idea. It's not an original idea, because eating is something you do everyday. It's even less of an original idea if you go to the same fast food restaurant everyday and order the same thing from the same menu. Perhaps it's time to use a small amount of creativity. Try eating somewhere new or tasting a new type of food. Creativity involves experimentation, experiencing new things, and discovering alternatives. As you learn to think creatively, the words *new* and *improved* will become commonly used terms.

While everyone can generate ideas with no problem whatsoever, not everyone allows him- or herself to develop creative or innovative ideas. There are a wide range of reasons (to be explored later) why people refuse to allow their creativity to flow freely. The trick to being a creative or innovative thinker is to look at things from a different perspective—to see the world differently, and then be willing to embrace change and possibly take risks as you implement your new ideas.

Generic ideas are very different from creative or innovative ideas. You already know how to think up ideas. Now, it's time to tap into your imagination as you discover how to brainstorm in order to generate creative and innovative ideas.

Look to Role Models for Inspiration

Everyone knows of at least a handful of creative or innovative thinkers whom they look up to, idolize, or consider role models. As you begin to master the art of creative thinking, look to these people for inspiration. Try to learn how they think and what inspires them. Try to replicate their success for yourself.

To begin, start by creating a list of at least five creative people you believe have already achieved success. These do not need to be people you know. They can be famous people, historical figures, corporate leaders, entertainers, artists, or even politicians.

As you list the five creative or innovative thinkers who truly impress you, consider what is it about each person that inspires you. What qualities do they possess that you could mimic or adopt into your own life? In the entertainment field, for example, some people you might consider inspirations include: Walt Disney, Gene Roddenberry (the creator of *Star Trek*), Jim Henson (creator of The Muppets), Alfred Hitchcock, George Lucas, Francis Ford Coppola, or Steven Speilberg. If you work in a specific industry, try listing people you look up to in that specific field.

List your five creative thinkers now.

1. _____

2. _____

3. _____

4. _____

5. _____

Using these five people as a starting point, do some research at the library or online and learn as much as you can about each of them. For example, what are their philosophies? What sparked their creativity? How did they successfully incorporate creative thinking into their work?

If you know the people on your list and have direct access to any of them, ask questions. As you learn about the people you admire because of their creativity, discover what qualities you can emulate to enhance your own creativity and success. Thus, as you begin tapping into your own creativity, you could ask yourself, "What would _____*[insert name]*_____ do when approaching this situation?" Having done some research, you should be able to discover and make educated guesses about how your role model might handle various situations you're now confronting. Use this knowledge as a starting point for your own inspiration and creativity.

Understanding the Terminology

Throughout this book, certain terminology, like *brainstorming, creative thinking*, and *innovative thinking* will be used somewhat interchangeably. Before moving forward, let's take a look at what some of these terms mean.

Brainstorming is a technique or activity used to encourage creative thinking and the generation of multiple ideas to address a specific problem or issue. Brainstorming is a process that can be done by a single person or in a group.

It is done to generate ideas—not to analyze or implement them. This process is sometimes referred to as *lateral thinking* because systematic techniques are used to address problems, sometimes using various unusual or unproven methods.

Creativity or *creative thinking* is a way of focusing your mind to generate new and innovative ideas that haven't been considered before. It's about tapping into a part of your brain that will allow you to see something from a different perspective or put a different spin on a problem or issue. Thinking is simply the process of thought. You can think about all types of ideas without being creative. Creative thinking or innovative thinking, however, is a thought process you engage in (alone or in a group) in order to generate new ideas and to think in a way that deliberately encourages new ideas to evolve. Creative thinking is also referred to as *divergent thinking* because traditional thought patterns are expanded upon.

Throughout this book, the concept of addressing a problem through creative thinking or brainstorming is addressed. A "problem," in this case, isn't necessarily something that needs to be fixed. The problem at hand could be an opportunity, a challenge, a question, a concern, or some other situation that could be improved upon by implementing new ideas. Any type of situation or issue that will benefit from a change to the current process can be thought of as a problem to be addressed by brainstorming.

For example, you might engage in a brainstorming session to generate new ideas for a product or service. In this case, the problem you're addressing is the need for new product/service ideas. Likewise, if you're a songwriter, you might brainstorm to develop the lyrics to go along with a musical composition you've created. In this case, the problem you're addressing is the need for lyrics. In some situations, you might brainstorm to discover new opportunities within your organization. For example, you might want to develop new ideas for marketing existing products or services, or create new ways of using an existing product so that it will appeal to a larger potential customer base.

Why Do We Need New Ideas?

New ideas help us evolve as a society and as individuals. They're what allow us to invent new things, improve upon existing things, and make our quality of life better. Some ideas are revolutionary, while some are new and innovative, but don't change the world.

The invention of the automobile, for example, was revolutionary. It changed the way people traveled from one place to another and put a lot of horses out of work. The release of Madonna's, Aerosmith's, or Garth Brook's latest single represented new and innovative ideas from a musical standpoint and provided enjoyment for millions of music lovers worldwide, but didn't change the way most of us lead our lives.

Every idea that is created has a purpose. To make brainstorming new ideas easier, it's always an excellent strategy to begin by defining a purpose and putting a label on it so that your purpose can easily be communicated to others.

Virtually all ideas are created to:

- Solve problems.

- Address an issue.

- Confront an obstacle.

- Make something better, cheaper, easier, or more fun.

Even a work of art or song is a solution to a problem that was conceived within the artist or songwriter's mind. Perhaps the artwork was created to make a statement or to convey a concept (no matter how vague).

Within the corporate world, new ideas are constantly needed in order to develop new products and services, improve upon existing ones, successfully market them, boost profits, cut costs, reduce waste, and enhance productivity, for example. If you're a parent of a young child, new ideas are constantly needed to keep your child from getting bored at home, or when you need a theme for his or her next birthday party. If you're a painter, even if you decide you want to paint an everyday object, like an apple, you need ideas in order to express your vision of that apple on the canvas.

An idea does not have to be revolutionary to be considered good or to have a positive impact on someone or something. An idea can build or improve upon already existing ideas, thus becoming an extension of the original idea.

Original Ideas

Original ideas are developed based on something totally new and innovative that has never been conceived of before. Inventors often come up with original ideas that have the potential to impact our lives—with new products, theories, or technologies, for example.

In your opinion, what are some of the most awesome inventions (developed from original ideas) introduced throughout our history? Take a moment and list your top 10 choices.

1. _____

2. _____

3. _____

4. _____

5. _____

6. _____

7. _____

8. _____

9. _____

10. _____

Depending on your own background and how you approached this question, your answers might have included: medicine, automobiles, computers, airplanes, radio, TV, the steam engine, transistors, electricity, or the telephone.

A truly original idea, something unlike anything anyone has ever come up with, is hard to come by. Most ideas, including many that you probably just listed, were somehow improvements to an existing idea. While television can be considered a totally original concept (the ability to transmit moving pictures and sound over the airways), it could be argued that television was an improvement to radio (which only transmitted sound).

Reworking Existing Ideas

Looking at the list you have just created, you should be able to see how certain major innovations and inventions were created as improvements upon other concepts or products, or in order to solve specific problems. Just because an idea is based upon another, or somehow improves upon another idea, it doesn't make your idea any less important or credible.

Throughout this book, you're going to be asked to participate in short exercises to help you enhance your creativity and brainstorming skills. Are you ready to give it a try? Go to your desk and grab an ordinary paper clip.

Obviously, a paper clip is a common office supply used to hold a small number of papers together. Using whatever capacity of creativity and brainstorming capabilities you possess right now, make a list of five other uses tor a paper clip. Take as long as you need, but stick to this exercise until it's completed.

The rules for this exercise are:

- Your ideas don't have to be practical.

- There are no right or wrong answers or solutions.

- There is no time limit.

- There is no such thing as a stupid response.

- There are no other rules in terms of what you do with the paper clip to develop your ideas.

Begin approaching this brainstorming session by defining the problem. In this case, you have a paper clip, and you need to come up with five creative things to do with it. Look at your paper clip from a different perspective, forgetting about its everyday use. Next, write down every idea, no matter how ridiculous or outrageous. Remember, when you're brainstorming, there's no such thing as a stupid, inappropriate, or bad idea.

Aside from holding together a few sheets of paper, what *could* a paper clip be used for?

1. _____

2. _____

3. _____

4. _____

5. _____

Are you finished? Do you have your list? How long did the exercise take? In case you're totally stuck, here are a few possible answers:

- Attach keys and use the paper clip as a keychain.

- Use the paper clip as a money clip instead of using a wallet.

- You could link paper clips together into a chain to make a necklace or bracelet.

- Stretch out a single paper clip and wrap it into a circle to create a ring for your finger.

✄ Stretch out and then rebend the paper clip into different shapes in order to create some type of stick figure, tiny statue, or artwork.

✄ Stretch out the paper clip and use it to push in the tiny reset button of your handheld PDA when it freezes.

Even if you weren't able to come up with five responses, hopefully you at least generated ideas for one or two things a paper clip could be used for. Congratulations! You just completed your first official brainstorming session. You just adapted someone else's idea—the invention of a paper clip—and expanded upon it. In this case, you might not have developed any revolutionary ideas or uses for a paper clip that will change the paper clip industry forever, but you did prove to yourself that you have the basic skills needed to brainstorm and develop your own ideas.

What It Means to "Think Outside the Box"

This phrase is so overused in corporate America, that most people no longer pay any attention to it. After all, what does it really mean? What is this hypothetical box anyway, and what's wrong with having your thoughts locked up inside of it?

What does the phrase "think outside the box" mean to you? Take a moment to consider it. From a creative thinking and brainstorming standpoint, this phrase could mean that all of our everyday ideas, the way we see things (our perspectives), and our ways of doing things, are all old, unoriginal, and generic. They're stale ideas that we stick to out of laziness, convenience, or not having a better solution. We're seeing things from the perspective of inside the hypothetical box only, and thus seeing things from only one point of view.

By simply stepping "outside of the box," our perspective instantly changes. We can see things differently and can take different approaches to the same problems, challenges, and issues that confront us every day. We can approach things using a different mindset and a new set of experiences, which will allow us to develop ideas that never came to mind before, simply because we never needed or wanted them to. New, creative, and innovative ideas are often generated simply by looking at or considering something in a totally different way.

Customizing an Idea to Meet Your Needs

Sometimes, generating a new idea isn't at all what you need to do in order to solve a particular problem or address a situation. There will be times when it's more appropriate and easier not to reinvent the wheel, but to take an already established idea and customize it to meet your specific needs.

For example, suppose you work for a Fortune 500 company and a memo gets circulated that employees are spending too much time using the Internet for frivolous purposes. This is lowering productivity. You're told to cut wasted Internet usage, save time, and become more productive.

After evaluating how and when you use the Internet at work, you determine that you're spending absolutely no time surfing the Web for entertainment or for personal reasons. You're not chatting with friends using an instant messaging program, planning your next vacation, or even playing online games.

In terms of your Internet usage, what's keeping you and your colleagues from being more productive is having to sort through the dozens of junk e-mail messages that show up in your inbox every day. In your inbox are those annoying spam messages and chain letter e-mails that contain jokes and other content that takes valuable time to read and respond to.

What can be done to achieve the company's objective, yet not impact your own productive Internet usage? One idea for employees is for them to simply stop surfing. (How unoriginal!) After some consideration and brainstorming, your idea is to incorporate the use of e-mail filtering software onto your company's network. This software could block 90 percent of the junk e-mail that's filling up the employees' inboxes. You could also issue a mandate that no chain e-mails should be circulated at work, unless they are work related. These new ideas will solve the overall problem and allow people to keep surfing the Web (for reasonable purposes). As a result, productivity goes up and everyone is happy. This is just one example of how one idea can be customized or modified to achieve the desired outcome in a faster, easier, and more acceptable way.

Customizing ideas is different from changing rules you're supposed to follow, unless those changes are authorized by superiors. In the right circumstances, however, rules *are* made to be broken, if the outcome is positive and the changes are acceptable to the rule makers as well as the rule followers.

Who Generates Those Really Big Ideas?

When you answer this question in your own mind, you might think of people like Albert Einstein, Thomas Edison, Bill Gates, or other world-famous inventors and innovative thinkers.

The truth is, however, most really great ideas in the world are generated by people just like you. The best ideas come from people who have the guts not only to express their creativity, to think differently, and to share their ideas with the world, but who are also willing to work hard to help people accept their ideas, implement them, and ultimately make them a reality.

It's true, it is the job of inventors, scientists, researchers, artists, writers, and musicians, for example, to spend much of their time thinking creatively. For everyday people, however, this is a skill that can become just one aspect of your everyday life. You don't need to be a genius like Albert Einstein or a skilled musician, artist, or writer to add creative thinking and brainstorming to your personal or professional skill set.

You Too Can Transform Your Ideas Into Reality

After you learn the secrets behind creative thinking and brainstorming, you'll discover that coming up with awesome ideas is only step one. To generate the tremendous results you're hoping for, you will need to analyze your ideas, choose the best ones, and then somehow implement your best ideas and make them a reality.

Yes, analyzing ideas and choosing the best ones are important, but there's a right time and a wrong time to be critical of your ideas (and the ideas generated by others). During the initial brainstorming phase, there should be no critique or analyzing of ideas. When you're brainstorming, quantity is more important than quality, in terms of the ideas you generate. Only after an abundance of ideas have been brought to the table do you want to go back and consider which ones are most suited to solving the problem at hand.

After analyzing your ideas and selecting the best ones, it will be time to establish a plan for implementing those ideas. Implementing an idea is very much like achieving any other goal in life. You'll want to set a clearly defined objective, establish a deadline, and then create a well-thought-out and organized plan for implementing each idea. This will include determining what needs to get done, figuring out the best way to get those things accomplished, and constantly working toward the ultimate implementation of your idea into whatever aspect of your life it applies to.

Basic project management, time management and organizational skills, as well as your personal motivation and perhaps the support of others, will all be needed to implement your ideas once you choose which ones are worth pursuing.

Leave Your Fear and Insecurity Behind!

Throughout this book, you will learn all sorts of strategies for becoming a creative thinker and discover ways to improve upon your brainstorming skills. You'll even have a chance to learn brainstorming and creative thinking techniques from well-known experts.

If you learn only one lesson from this book, however, it should be that you must never be afraid to think creatively or worry about what other people will ultimately think of your ideas. Becoming a master brainstormer means not being afraid to be vulnerable as you develop and convey your thoughts and ideas to others.

Fear is what sets apart brilliant thinkers from average thinkers. Especially during your idea creation or brainstorming sessions, you can't ever worry about an idea being too stupid, too outrageous, not feasible, not accepted by your peers, or flat out wrong. As you evaluate ideas later, you can weed out the ones that won't work. As a brainstormer, your first job is to come up with ideas—lots of them.

This concept of overcoming fear and personal insecurity will be reiterated several times and in different ways throughout this book, because it's the primary reason why people never achieve their true potential when it comes to brainstorming and creative thinking.

What's Coming Up?

Brain Storm was written to provide you with practical advice and strategies that you will ultimately be able to incorporate into your life with minimal effort. A lot of technical and scientific research has been done about creativity, brainstorming, and how ideas are generated. There are also many philosophical theories involved with this area of study. That's not, however, what this book is all about. It's not a textbook offering the theories and scientific research behind how ideas are generated and what makes the brain work the way it does. This book is for people who want to be more creative in their thinking and who wish to apply what they learn right away. In the next chapter, we'll take a look at what inspires creativity. Then, beginning in Chapter 3, you'll start learning how to brainstorm.

As helpful as the step-by-step directions and interactive exercises offered in the first eight chapters will be, the interviews featured in the later part of this book will allow you to learn from the firsthand experiences of well-known people (and people from well-known companies) who have achieved success in large part due to their creative thinking and brainstorming abilities. What you can learn from these people (using them as role models) can be extremely useful in your own life as you begin to apply what you learn in the early chapters.

So get ready to pop the top on your brain and mix things up a bit. You're about to learn how to see things differently and approach problems and issues in a whole new way!

CHAPTER 2

The Anatomy of an Idea

Before you begin generating those awesome ideas, this chapter will help you understand where ideas originate. You'll also be encouraged to examine your own life and start determining what inspires your creativity right now.

Implementing New Ideas Can Improve All Aspects of Your Life

As you already know, the purpose for generating new ideas, being creative, and brainstorming is to solve problems, address issues, confront obstacles, or make something better, cheaper, easier, or more fun. Well, these situations come up in all aspects of your life—not just work.

Perhaps your reason for reading this book is to improve your ability to think creatively ("outside of the box") at work. Have you been given a mandate from your superiors to develop new products or services, enhance your company's marketing efforts, generate new customers, boost profits, reduce waste, cut costs, make day-to-day operations run smoother, or become more productive—but the way you're thinking right now isn't leading to the ideas needed to make your objectives happen?

In your personal life, do you have a hobby into which you'd like to delve deeper, such as painting, sculpture, playing an instrument, drawing, singing, knitting, gardening, cooking, home improvement, stamp collecting, or scrap booking, but don't have the time, energy, or what you perceive to be enough creative talent to properly pursue it? Is time too short to properly juggle your career as well as your family life? Are you so stressed out at home as a result of work, that spending quality time with loved ones has become a challenge?

What about the financial aspects of your life? Do you have savings that could be working harder for you in terms of your investment strategies? Are you trying to live on a tight budget, but find this isn't possible with all of your expenses? Are you dealing with ever growing credit card debt? Do you need to plan your retirement, but at this time in your life, can't even cover your day-to-day expenses, much less expenses that you'll have 10, 20, 30, or more years from now? Do you need to take a different, more creative approach to managing your finances so you can make your money stretch farther or pay off debt?

Once you begin defining what specific problems, issues, concerns, and obstacles you face in your life, one at a time, and then consider what solutions you'd like to achieve, you can use your creativity and brainstorming skills to examine each thing from many different perspectives. Then, analyze those ideas, and determine the best course of action to follow. Later, you can implement those new ideas, even if they take you in a totally different direction from where you're headed now.

As you'll discover, once issues, problems, and concerns are pinpointed, some will require only minimal brainstorming and no radical changes to the status quo to improve the situation. Others things, however, may require you to think radically, make drastic changes to the way things are being done, take risks, and not be afraid to be vulnerable as you generate ideas that could lead to tremendous results. What's actually required in terms of change and alternative thinking will become obvious as you begin considering each problem individually and think about what the desired outcome needs to be.

After you begin using your creativity and brainstorming abilities often, to achieve the specific purpose(s) you began reading this book for, you'll begin to tap these new skills, almost subconsciously, in all aspects of your life. It will most likely be a gradual process, so be sure you allow this to happen without being too critical of yourself. Embrace the changes in the way you think and utilize this to your advantage.

Understanding Your Brain

Your brain is the most complex organ in your body. It's the master control center, responsible for everything your body does, from breathing to thinking. At any given second, the human brain is handling thousands of simultaneous tasks, allowing you to stay alive and experience the world around you.

Scientists, doctors, and researchers throughout history have dedicated their lives to the study of the human brain, yet they've only begin to scratch the surface when it comes to truly understanding how this amazing organ operates. The study of the brain is called *neuroscience* or *neurobiology*.

To become a creative thinker and master the art of brainstorming, you don't really need a thorough understanding of how each of the more than 100 billion nerve cells (neurons) in your brain work, but knowing the basics can help you better tap into the lesser-used areas of your brain in order to achieve success in whatever you set out to accomplish.

There's a widely accepted theory that the human brain can be divided into two primary areas, or hemispheres. This left brain/right brain theory was developed in the early 1970s by Dr. Roger Sperry from the University of California.

According to the left brain/right brain theory, the right side of the brain controls creativity. It's more active than the left side when a human is involved in such creative activities as listening to music, drawing, daydreaming, and absorbing color, graphics, movement, and rhythm.

While the right brain is good for being creative, the left brain comes in handy when you're thinking logically, rationally, objectively, or analytically. The left brain is used more when you use language, write, read, solve math problems, or process information. Thus, human thought can be divided into two distinct modes. Right now, as you read this book, you're using your left brain more than your right brain, because you're reading the words and processing their meanings.

Now, take a moment and close your eyes. With your eyes closed, think about your favorite vacation destination, such as a beautiful tropical beach on a warm and sunny day. Can you picture the sand, ocean, warm breeze, and seashells in your mind? If so, you just used the right side of your brain! Congratulations, you have the ability to be creative!

As you master the ability to brainstorm and become a creative thinker in all aspects of your life, you'll ultimately want to use your right brain in conjunction with your left brain, so as you develop awesome ideas, you can later analyze and implement them.

Based upon Dr. Sperry's research, it's believed that most people focus more on using one side of their brain than the other. This could account for why some people are good at math, for example, while others are more creative and artistic, relying on their feelings and emotions to drive their actions.

Everyone uses both sides of their brain on an ongoing basis. Ideally, you want to discover how to use both sides of your brain equally in order to tap into your brain's true potential. Those who use both sides of their brain, without a subconscious emphasis on utilizing their left brain or right brain together, are called "whole brained." This is ultimately what you'd like to achieve as you begin tapping into your creativity and begin developing creative thinking skills to be used in all aspects of your life.

Where Ideas Come From

Your brain is an amazing thing. It's where all of your ideas are generated, but it isn't necessarily your brain that inspires itself to be creative. Your experiences, what you see, hear, feel, taste, and smell, who you meet, where you go, and how you spend your time all act as triggers and help you make associations so your brain can generate ideas and brainstorm.

The more experiences you have and the more you're exposed to, the more your brain will have to work with when you encourage it to brainstorm. Even in the best of circumstances, however, *triggers* are often useful to get your brain thinking about a specific thing from a different perspective.

A trigger is simply an idea, object, word, phrase, sound, image, taste, smell, or anything else that causes your brain to think differently about the situation you're brainstorming about. In some situations, using a random trigger and then making associations between the trigger and what you're brainstorming about will lead to new ideas.

If you're using random words as triggers, a noun (a person, place, or thing) that is not related to what you're thinking about typically works the best. The human brain automatically works to organize its thoughts. It's able to quickly make connections. Thus, any random word has the power to stimulate ideas on the subject at hand. Keep your mind open and allow the associations created from the trigger to take place.

The purpose of a trigger is to help you follow a trail of thinking that you ordinarily would not have pursued. Your mind is always working to make associations and connections. It has the ability to think in a linear fashion, like a computer, but also to work associatively in order to string seemingly random ideas and concepts together.

A trigger can be useful in helping your mind unlock ideas. As you consider the trigger, think about what words come to mind, how it makes you feel, and consider all aspects of it using all of your senses. Many people use music, pictures, and life experiences as triggers when brainstorming. In Chapter 3, the use of triggers will be explored in greater detail.

Aside from triggers, there are many different exercises and activities in which you can engage to spark your creative thinking process and help you brainstorm. Investing the time to experiment with these activities and see which ones work best for you when dealing with specific types of situations will be beneficial. Part of becoming a good brainstormer and a creative thinker is learning how to use the tools at your disposal to generate the ideas you want and need. Several brainstorming and creativity exercises will be discussed in Chapter 4.

It's easy to accept things as status quo and think along the lines of something that's already the norm and widely accepted. It's slightly more challenging to look at that same thing from a totally different perspective and foresee a more grandiose outcome as a result.

If you're worried that creative thinking isn't something you're capable of doing, you're wrong! Anytime you dream at night, daydream during the day, or fantasize about something, you're thinking creatively. When you read a novel, for example, and pictures of the characters you're reading about form in your head, that's a form of creative thinking. When you're in a business meeting or in class and you randomly start doodling on the paper in front of you, that is also a form of creative thinking and expression.

What Environments Inspire Your Creativity?

In terms of creativity, people tend to work best in environments where they:

- Are comfortable—both emotionally and physically.
- Are not stressed out.
- Are able to relax.
- Can avoid constant distractions.
- Have the ability to focus on the task at hand.
- Don't have fear of rejection, ridicule, or criticism.

The environment in which you choose to tap into your creativity, whether for business or pleasure, is important. Many artists, for example, are most comfortable working in the studio they create for themselves.

Think about what inspires your own creativity. Next, establish an environment for yourself that is conducive to being creative or brainstorming. This might mean adjusting the lighting in the room, playing music in the background, controlling the temperature, opening the windows, making yourself comfortable by sitting on a couch (as opposed to an uncomfortable chair at your regular desk), wearing your "lucky" outfit, or somehow blocking out outside noises and distractions.

Be sure that whatever brainstorming tools you plan to utilize, such as a paper and pen, whiteboards, computer software, or artist supplies, are readily available in ample quantities. You don't want to interrupt a productive brainstorming session and lose your train of thought in order to look for a pen that works, for example.

When creating the perfect environment to tap into your creativity and brainstorm, consider the following:

- Lighting in the room.
- Temperature.
- Comfort of the furniture.
- Ambiance of your surroundings.
- Noise level.
- Availability of the tools and resources you'll need.
- Size of the space. (Is the area large enough to move around or for several people to brainstorm with you?)
- Potential disruptions and distractions.

How would you describe the perfect environment in which you believe you'd flourish from a creative standpoint?

_____

_____

_____

_____

_____

_____

_____

_____

_____

The environment you create will probably evolve over time as you figure out how you work best. Once you've established the best possible environment to spur your creativity and ability to think clearly, consider the best time of day to do your brainstorming.

Are you a morning person, an afternoon person, or a night owl? When do the best ideas typically come to you? When are you the most alert and able to think clearly? What time of day do you have the most energy? To maximize the results of your efforts, you'll ideally want to work when you know you're most productive based upon past experiences.

Obviously, you won't always be able to work in an ideal environment. You might be stuck at your desk in the middle of a busy office or forced to work under a tight deadline, for example. There are going to be times when you'll need to make compromises, but try to stick as closely to your perfect environment as possible. For example, even if you're forced to work in your busy office, put on music in the background—music that you know inspires or relaxes you.

It's always ideal to utilize the best possible environment whenever you can, especially when you're first starting to master your brainstorming skills. Ultimately, you'll probably discover that the "perfect environment" you create for brainstorming is also an ideal place for you to be productive in other aspects of your life.

Avoid Things That Block Your Creativity

Even people who have mastered the art of brainstorming or who are considered to be some of the most creative or innovative thinkers in the world sometimes have trouble achieving their objectives. Writers experience "writer's block" for example. As you'll discover in Chapters 4 and 5, there are many things you can do if you get stuck when brainstorming or trying to tap into your creativity.

Obviously, it's best to do everything possible in advance, to avoid creative blockages from taking place. When you're preparing to kick off a brainstorming session, take a few minutes before you get started to make a list of all the potential distractions you might encounter.

On pages 30 and 31 are two lists of potential distractions and possible solutions. Embellish upon them as needed.

While many of the potential distractions you might experience in the workplace are also potential distractions at home, listed are some additional things you might want to avoid so that they don't hamper your creative thinking or brainstorming.

Once you know what potential distractions might keep you from achieving your brainstorming goals, take steps to keep these distractions from happening before you get started.

Workplace Distractions	Potential Solutions
Telephone calls.	Turn off your ringer. Let voice mail or your assistant answer the phone.
People popping into the office.	Close, and if necessary, lock your office door. You might consider doing your brainstorming outside of your regular office—in a conference room, for example.
Other work.	Make sure you schedule time for your brainstorming session, so that other work doesn't need to be done at the same time. Finish whatever work you can in advance, or schedule time later to complete it.
Meetings you must attend.	Time management and organizational skills are critical. Make sure you schedule ample time to do your brainstorming so it doesn't overlap with your other professional commitments.
The right tools and supplies aren't available.	Determine what you'll need in advance, in terms of office supplies, brainstorming tools, and other resources. Bring the necessary items into your brainstorming session with you. Make sure you have enough for everyone and that you won't run out of vital items, such as pens, paper, and junk food (refreshments).
Too much noise.	Finding a quieter environment will be best, but you could always wear earplugs (if you're working alone), or add calming music to the environment to help you relax. Bose Corporation sells QuietComfort noise reduction headsets. Wearing these Walkman-like headsets will both reduce the noise in an otherwise loud environment and allow you to listen to soothing music. (For more information about this product, call 1-800-999-2673 or visit: *www.bose.com/noise_reduction/qc_headset.*)

Home Distractions	Potential Solutions
Noisy kids.	Send them outside or to a friend's house to play. You could also hire a babysitter.
Loud or disruptive pets.	A dog barking or even a cat jumping all over your home office and rubbing against your leg when you're trying to concentrate could be distracting. Keep the pets out of the room you'll be working in.
Poor work environment.	Unless you have a home office or studio set up, finding a place where you can work alone in your home might prove difficult. After all, you want to be away from other people, as well as dirty dishes, laundry, and other household clutter that might keep you from focusing on the task at hand. In the space you have available, try to create the best possible work environment by adjusting the lighting, temperature, background music, and comfort level.

Additional Distractions	Potential Solutions
_____	_____
_____	_____
_____	_____
_____	_____
_____	_____
_____	_____
_____	_____
_____	_____

It All Starts With Brainstorming!

Becoming a creative thinker and applying these skills to your personal, professional, and financial life involves several important phases, including:

- 🗱 Identifying and articulating a problem, challenge, issue, or objective.

- 🗱 Brainstorming ideas to address the situation at hand.

- 🗱 Analyzing and evaluating the ideas, then choosing the best (not necessarily the most feasible or traditional ideas).

- 🗱 Implementing your idea(s).

Later, you'll discover that each of these phases needs to be addressed separately and requires a different way of thinking. When it comes to actually generating new and innovative ideas, it's the brainstorming phase that will be the most useful. However, you first need to have a good understanding of what you're attempting to accomplish.

Part of brainstorming involves generating a wide range of ideas—some practical and some totally wacky and outrageous. Sometimes, with a little tweaking, it will be the most outrageous ideas that eventually evolve into the very best ideas for addressing the situation at hand, by using a totally different (perhaps radical) approach.

Chapter 3 focuses on the first two phases for implementing a creative-thinking strategy—identifying and articulating a problem, challenge, issue or objective, then brainstorming ideas to address the situation at hand. There are many ways to brainstorm and various strategies you can incorporate to generate better results. You'll discover many of these exercises in Chapters 3 and 4. Get ready to jump-start your creative thinking and brainstorming skills!

CHAPTER 3

Brainstorming 101

Brainstorming is an activity people from all walks of life use to generate ideas in a relatively quick and organized manner. It's when you put your creative thinking skills to the test in order to conceive multiple ideas that will potentially help you solve a particular problem or address a situation.

Why brainstorm? Here are some general objectives:

- To generate ideas and possible solutions for addressing an issue or problem.

- To cover the full range of possibilities when addressing an issue or problem.

- To stimulate creativity when addressing an issue or problem.

- To promote a more organized approach to problem-solving for yourself or within your organization.

- To encourage the "anything is possible" mentality when creating a flow of ideas.

Where did brainstorming come from? In a way, brainstorming can be looked at as a type of psychological technique adapted from psychotherapist Sigmund Freud back in the early 1900s. As part of his therapy, Freud would have his clients lay on a couch and "free associate" the ideas that came into their head. He would later analyze these thoughts and ideas with the client.

People can brainstorm alone or in groups and will be driven by countless personal and professional motivations and inspirations. Writers, artists, and musicians, for example, all use brainstorming and creativity to create their works. Business people use brainstorming to develop new approaches for work-related problems.

There are no predefined rules for brainstorming. Everyone does this differently. For example, some people close themselves off in a room, dim the lights, turn on music, and focus on finding creative and new solutions for a situation at hand. Others, as you'll read about in Chapter 11, set off on 50-mile bicycle treks in order to clear their minds, eliminate distractions, and see things from a different perspective.

Participating in a brainstorming session provides you with a forum to tap into your creativity for a specific purpose. However, you don't need to limit yourself in terms of when or how you utilize your creativity and ability to generate new ideas. Creative thinking should become a skill you incorporate into every aspect of your life on an ongoing basis.

It doesn't matter what approach you take when brainstorming, as long as you follow a few basic strategies to focus your energies on the task at hand. This chapter explores the art of brainstorming and offers strategies to help you get started.

Always Identify Your Goal, Problem, Opportunity, or Objective

Before you can begin a productive brainstorming session, you must know why you're brainstorming and what you'd like the outcome to be. Without a defined purpose, whatever time you spend brainstorming won't be as productive as it could be. In defining your problem, goal, opportunity, or objective, always be as specific as possible. This will give you a basic starting point. For example, a retail business might brainstorm with the goal of generating 10 new marketing ideas that will boost sales in time for the holidays.

For such a goal, some of the things to consider in advance include: what has and has not worked in the past, your target consumer group, budget limitations you might have, and what image you're trying to convey to the public through your marketing efforts.

As you embark on your brainstorming session with the goal of generating new marketing strategies, some of the ideas might include (in no particular order):

1. Invite Santa to visit the store.

2. Promote a raffle or sweepstakes and offer an awesome prize.

3. Have a pre-Christmas sale.

4. Try radio advertising as opposed to just newspaper advertising.

5. For your newspaper ads, try a larger size ad and/or add color.

6. Extend shopping hours for the weeks prior to Christmas.

7. Kick off a "buy-two-get-one-free" promotion.

8. Add a selection of new products to inventory.

9. Implement a sidewalk sale to clear out older inventory.

10. Coordinate a celebrity appearance at your store.

A manufacturing company might have a goal to develop ideas for a new product. In such a case, you might ask yourself:

- What type of new product is needed or wanted, or what category should the product fit into?

- What features or functions are important?

- Who is the intended target consumer?

- What problem do you want the new product to solve for the buyer?

- What demand are you trying to fill?

- What market are you trying to break into?

When you consider brainstorming as a problem-solving tool, there are many ways to look at and identify a problem. As far as brainstorming and creative thinking is concerned, a problem doesn't necessarily need to be something that requires *fixing*. It could represent:

- A need that should or could be filled (such as an idea for a new product or service).

- A new opportunity that could be exploited (for example, breaking into a new marketplace with an existing product and creating a demand for it).

- Something that could be improved upon (the holiday season marketing efforts of your company, for example).

- A way to overcome an obstacle (such as a new method for marketing a product in order to beat the competition).

If you're an artist, your objective may be to create a new work of art based upon a certain theme or concept. As a writer, you may brainstorm to develop the plot for a new novel or a topic for a poem. The possibilities for why you might brainstorm are limitless.

The Pre-Brainstorming Questionnaire

Each time you set out to brainstorm, ask yourself these questions, even if the answers seem obvious:

✗ What is your primary goal or objective?

_____

_____

_____

_____

_____

✗ What problem are you trying to solve? (Keep in mind that a problem doesn't necessarily need to be something that requires *fixing*.)

_____

_____

_____

_____

_____

✗ What do you want the outcome to be?

_____

_____

_____

_____

_____

✗ What brainstorming process will you use to achieve this objective? What creative activities or exercises will be utilized? What tools will be used?

_____

_____

_____

_____

_____

✗ Who will be invited to participate in the brainstorming session? What unique skills, experience, or knowledge does each person offer? Why is each person being invited to participate?

_____

_____

_____

_____

Once you've identified what you're trying to achieve through brainstorming, create the perfect environment in which you or your team would work.

✗ Describe the ideal location and environment where the brainstorming session will be held. Will you use someone's office, the conference room, or some other location? What will the mood of the environment be? Will food and beverages be served?

_____

_____

_____

_____

_____

Let The Brainstorming Begin!

One reason why brainstorming works so well is because it encourages participants to suggest many ideas, without putting limits on the types of ideas generated—limits based on such things as cost, practicality, accuracy, or originality. The goal of any brainstorming session is to put one's analytical thinking on hold and allow the right side of your brain to temporarily control your thoughts so your brain focuses more on creative ideas instead of coming up with logical ones.

Brainstorming isn't just about coming up with generic ideas—it's about coming up with new, cutting edge, or innovative ideas using a series of activities or exercises to promote a way of thinking that your brain might not be used to.

Once you've determined what the goal of your brainstorming session is, determine the best approach to take in order to achieve your specific objective. In Chapter 4, you'll learn about brainstorming activities and exercises designed to promote creativity and innovative thinking. Utilizing one or two (or more) of these activities may prove valuable.

In addition, however, you need to decide what other brainstorming tools you plan to utilize and make sure they're available. At the very least, people involved in the brainstorming session should be equipped with paper and a pen to write down ideas, thoughts, concepts, etc. Once you get started, ideas could be conceived at a very fast pace, so be sure there's someone on hand to write down everything. You'll have to do this yourself if you're brainstorming alone.

Along with having a goal or objective, the right environment, and the proper brainstorming tools on hand, the next thing you'll need before actually getting started is some type of deadline or parameters for the brainstorming session.

Because most people don't work well under tight deadlines or intense pressure, a time deadline does not typically work best for brainstorming. Thus, setting your brainstorming deadline and parameters to be, for example, to generate the perfect new product idea within a three hour brainstorming session probably isn't the best approach.

You'll typically have better results if you take away the time element of your deadline and establish a goal for a brainstorming session, such as generating 10 new product ideas in whatever time that takes (within reason, of course). With a time deadline, you run the risk of your mind freezing up. Deadlines often cause pressure, especially when you know you need two or three more ideas to reach your goal of 10, but the clock is ticking down too quickly. Although, when developing deadlines or parameters for a brainstorming session, it is important to be realistic, based on your personal (or work-related) situation.

Don't forget, the goal of any brainstorming session is simply to generate ideas, not evaluate or implement them. That comes later. For now, focus your energies on coming up with ideas that could somehow address the problem you're trying to solve or the issue you're confronting.

Once the brainstorming begins, consider the topic at hand. To get started, force yourself to come up with at least a few totally outrageous ideas. Don't even consider anything that's remotely practical. This will force you to open your mind and forget about barriers.

Next, look at the problem at hand from as many different perspectives as possible, utilizing *all* of your senses—sight, hearing, taste, smell, and touch. Use whatever triggers are necessary to get your mind working and start writing things down. Ask questions, starting with the basics (*who, what, where, when, why,* and *how.*)

Once you get things rolling, you'll find your brainstorming sessions will snowball as your mind will almost automatically begin making new connections and associations—some based upon your outrageous and wacky ideas.

Utilize creative thinking during your brainstorming sessions. This means you might combine new ideas with existing ideas in innovative ways. The brainstorming session should act as a forum to think creativity as opposed to analytically.

Keep your brainstorming session going until you've achieved your goal or deadline. For example, if the goal is to generate 10 new ideas for something, don't quit after just three or four really good ideas are created. Stay focused and avoid distractions. In the next section, we'll focus on strategies for brainstorming alone. Later in this chapter, the concept of brainstorming in groups will be addressed.

Brainstorming Alone: Just You and Your Ideas

Engaging in a brainstorming session all by yourself has its benefits and drawbacks. One major benefit is that you don't have to worry about other people judging your ideas as they're created. You're free to go wherever your brain takes you as you utilize the brainstorming techniques described in Chapter 4 to generate ideas. Another benefit is that you can create the ideal environment for you personally, and not have to worry about the needs of other people. If you want music on in the background, for example, you can pick the type of music and the volume.

Another benefit to brainstorming alone is that you can set your own schedule, without having to worry about fitting your session into other peoples' hectic day. You can take advantage of commuting time, brainstorm in the shower, at home in bed, in your office (behind closed doors), during your lunch hour, or while sitting quietly in a park.

The drawback to brainstorming alone is that you're using just one mind to generate ideas. You have nobody's ideas to build upon. You must also create your own inspirations. In a group situation, you might find that a word someone says or a thought someone conveys will cause your brain to see an issue from a different perspective and thus generate a new idea. Without the immediate interaction of others, the ideas you will ultimate generate will stem only from your own experiences and knowledge as well as the thoughts and preconceived notions of whatever it is you're brainstorming about.

Even artists, musicians, and writers sometimes work with collaborators, simply to infuse fresh ideas into the work they do. In a business situation, you could always brainstorm alone and then compare your ideas and thoughts with those who have also brainstormed about the same topic. As you compare notes later (when it comes time to analyze ideas and choose the best ones) you could exchange ideas and perhaps generate new ones by merging the ideas created by multiple people.

Brainstorming with a Group

When gathering a group to brainstorm, keep in mind that there's a big difference between a group and a crowd. If too many people are involved, tracking ideas and interaction between group members will become difficult and confusing. Choose a group size that's comfortable, say between two and 10 people.

In a group situation, brainstorming is used for collecting ideas. However, the ideas you all generate will be based upon the experiences, perspectives, and viewpoints of multiple people. Thus, if one person generates a good idea, two others might quickly come up with a way to build upon or improve that initial idea.

To get people warmed up and ready to begin working together, it's always a good strategy to start off a group brainstorming session by having everyone engage in some type of creative and fun exercise or activity that will break the ice and get people in the right frame of mind.

For example, give each person three minutes to create the most outrageous or humorous idea possible that relates to the situation, then pass the idea to the person next to them and have that person embellish the idea in two minutes or less, making it even more outlandish, yet still relevant to the problem at hand in some way.

For a group brainstorming session to work properly, everyone in the group must be able to express his or her ideas freely. If anyone feels afraid or intimidated, this will hamper your efforts.

In addition, there should be someone who works as the group moderator or facilitator. The person leading the brainstorming session doesn't necessarily need to be a manager or someone in an executive level position. It could be a peer or even an outside *brainstorming facilitator*—someone whose job it is to work as a consultant and manage brainstorming sessions, without actually participating in the idea creation process. This group leader or moderator should have several predefined responsibilities, including:

- Creating the brainstorming environment in advance (preparing the room and supplying the appropriate tools, such as paper and pens, to everyone).

- Making sure everyone understands the objective or goal and has the necessary background information about the problem that is trying to be solved.

- Keeping everyone focused on the task at hand.

- Recording all ideas that are generated.

- Posting all ideas created during a session for everyone to see and build upon.

- Insuring that nobody puts down, rejects, or analyzes an idea too soon (during the brainstorming session).

- Keeping the participants motivated.

- Making sure everyone in the group is heard, feels appreciated, and has a chance to participate in a non-judgmental atmosphere.

- Imposing deadlines or objectives for the brainstorming session. Deadlines and objectives should be explained in advance to all of the participants. It's the leader's job to insure that the deadlines or objectives are achieved.

- Rewarding (with verbal praise or some other incentive) those people who generate the best ideas, show initiative, or demonstrate the best enthusiasm.

- ⚡ Communicating to the group that all ideas are welcome, no matter how outrageous or wacky.

- ⚡ Maintaining order. Make sure everyone doesn't shout out at once.

The 12 Rules for Brainstorming

Whether you're brainstorming alone or in a group, the following 12 rules will help you achieve success.

1. Determine your objective or identify a problem. Until you truly understand why you are brainstorming and what you want the outcome to be, there's no point in generating ideas. If someone doesn't fully understand the problem, the challenge of creating a solution is even greater.

2. Establish rules and stick to them. For example, once you make it clear that no ideas will be judged during the brainstorming session, don't get caught in the common trap of thinking about the new ideas and saying, "Well that won't work, because…" or "That idea is totally impractical, because…"

3. Set goals or limits. The limits or parameters for a brainstorming session can relate to the duration of the session or the number of ideas you want to collect. Don't simply quit brainstorming at the first (or second or third) natural lull in the flow of ideas. If there is a lull, utilize a trigger or brainstorming technique (described in Chapter 4) to jump-start your efforts. Once you start, don't quit or allow yourself to get distracted until your goal or session parameter has been achieved. If you're looking for 10 new ideas, don't quit after the first great one or two ideas are generated.

4. No idea is too stupid. Be outrageous! This is one of the golden rules of brainstorming. You might come up with a totally off-the-wall idea that could never work, but that outrageous idea, once you think about its positive aspects, could lead you to an entirely new line of thinking.

5. Don't rush the process. Generating new ideas isn't a race. You can't necessarily say you're going to generate the next big idea in 30 minutes or one hour. Once you get things rolling, allow the ideas to flow. Keep building upon those ideas until you have enough to work with and believe you'll be able to choose the best ideas to implement as plausible and workable solutions to the problem at hand.

6. Don't judge your ideas too early. The brainstorming session, as you already know, is for generating new ideas—not for analyzing those ideas. Save the analytical thinking for later.

7. Generate excitement and enthusiasm. People can only be creative when they are in a positive frame of mind. It's the group leader's job to keep the participants in the brainstorming session motivated, upbeat, positive, and focused on the issue(s) at hand.

8. Build on other people's ideas. New and totally original ideas are awesome, but sometimes the best solution to the problem at hand is simply an improvement or modification to an already existing idea. Don't worry about being too original or not original enough while brainstorming—just focus on generating ideas.

9. Quantity counts when brainstorming. It's always better to be able to choose from 10, 20, 30, or more ideas generated from a brainstorming session than just a handful. Even if 99 percent of the ideas generated don't turn out to be useful, coming up with them will keep your brain moving in different directions and force you to consider things from different perspectives.

10. Don't be afraid. If you fear rejection or failure, you're more apt to experience it. In the brainstorming phase, understand that all ideas are important and worthwhile. If you believe you have a lot to contribute and don't worry about what others might think of your ideas, you're more apt to generate really great ideas that are creative.

11. Look at things from different perspectives. Use whatever tools are necessary, including your own five senses, to see things from different points of view. Your education, experiences, and background knowledge can also be utilized. Sometimes, your brain will help you make strange connections that will lead to incredible ideas.

12. Utilize brainstorming exercises or triggers when things get tough. Brainstorming isn't always easy. There will be times when your brain has trouble generating the ideas you're looking for. In these situations, don't quit! Instead, jump-start the brainstorming process by utilizing one or more of the exercises, activities, or triggers described in Chapter 4. Making associations between the task at hand and a random word trigger, for example, will often help to formulate new ideas.

There's Still More To Do!

Brainstorming ideas can be a fun and rewarding process, but it can also be a frustrating, time consuming, and challenging one, depending on the task at hand and how creative you allow yourself to be. As you already know, simply generating a bunch of ideas is only the first step toward success.

Once you've formulated ideas, you need to take a step back and think about them analytically. Only after the brainstorming session has come to an end is it appropriate to start judging your ideas and evaluating them based on their feasibility and merit. Chapter 6 focuses on various ways to analyze your ideas.

After hand picking your very best ideas for solving the problem at hand, you'll need to properly implement them in order to achieve the tremendous results you're looking for. Strategies for implementing your best ideas are offered in Chapter 7. In the next chapter, however, you're about to learn specific exercises for enhancing your creativity and helping you to brainstorm.

CHAPTER 4

Creative Thinking and Brainstorming Exercises

You're in the process of learning new skills. This learning process takes practice. Once you discover how the creative thinking and brainstorming process works, you'll be able to apply these skills to many aspects of your life, practically without thinking about it. To reach a point where this can happen, however, you need to exercise the creative elements in your brain and force yourself to think creatively, as opposed to strictly analytically.

This chapter is divided into several sections. The first section will focus on activities and exercises you can do as part of your everyday life in order to practice using your creative thinking skills. Keep in mind that part of being creative involves opening yourself up to the world around you, taking in new information, and looking at everyday things from a different perspective. As an ongoing strategy, you'll want to expose yourself to new experiences. Some of the exercises in this first section are designed to do this in a subtle way.

Later in this chapter, you'll discover strategies to help you think more creatively on your own (brainstorm) and successfully engage in brainstorming sessions (in a group) when the goal is to generate multiple ideas that relate to a specific problem you've identified and now need to solve. Don't forget that "problem," in this case, is used as a broad term that could include identifying an opportunity, a goal, or something that needs to be improved upon or fixed.

Everyday Things You Can Do to Become a Creative Thinker

Chances are, your life is pretty busy, especially if you're juggling a personal life (family) and a professional life (career). Learning to be a more creative thinker will help you approach the challenges you encounter in different ways, which will typically allow you to develop better solutions and improve your life.

As you're learning to utilize your ability to think creatively, it's important to keep practicing. It's like any other skill, such as playing a musical instrument. If you don't practice and keep trying to perfect your skill, you won't improve.

The following section contains some fun and easy activities you can do throughout your normal day, such as when you have a break at work, when you're driving, or when you're at home enjoying your free time. You can do many of these activities alone, or you can invite other participants to join in. Ultimately, the objectives of these activities are to broaden what you're exposed to in your day-to-day life, to look at things from a different perspective, and to practice thinking creatively.

Train Your Brain to Be More Creative

These exercises are described in no particular order, so choose whichever ones you feel the most comfortable with and start incorporating them into your life. The new things you experience will help to inspire your creativity and assist you in generating new and better ideas. After you finish reading this section, there's no better time than the present to get started. Choose any of the following exercises and give it a try!

✓ Read Different Newspapers and Magazines

If you're an avid reader of your local newspaper, spend a few days reading a newspaper with a different focus, such as *USA Today* or *The Wall Street Journal*. Then go to the newsstand and purchase three or four magazines you don't typically read, and read them from cover to cover. The magazines can focus on any topic, serious or not. Do this exercise once per month.

To take this exercise to a higher level and make it more effective, read magazines you'd never otherwise consider reading, either because they're not targeted to you or because you know nothing about the topic. Depending on your interests, you might pick up fashion, crafting, travel, health, computer, sports, or physical fitness magazines. As you read them, try to put yourself in the shoes of the target audience for the magazine and see things from their perspective.

Also, as you read the magazine, see if you can adopt and apply ideas and other people's solutions you read about to your own situation. For example, if an issue of *Businessweek* profiles a company that solved a particular problem in its industry, see if you can apply that same logic to your business.

✗ Watch a Different Type of TV Show at Least Once per Week

Some people are fans of sitcoms, one-hour dramas, movies, game shows, news magazine shows, or soap operas. At least once per week, pick a few shows you wouldn't typically be interested in and watch them in their entirety.

For example, you could expand your knowledge of current events by watching news programs or cable news networks such as CNN, Fox News, or MSNBC, or newsmagazine shows such as 20/20, Dateline NBC, and 60 Minutes.

Even if it's purely for entertainment purposes, once per week, watch some other type of program, such as a sitcom or a game show, instead of your usual choice. Juggle your television watching habits. Again, the idea is to expand your horizons and be exposed to new ways of thinking, other perspectives, and different ideas.

✗ Go Somewhere Different on Vacation

Whether you're planning a weekend getaway or a two-week trip, select a destination you've never been to and make the most out of your time by exploring, meeting new people, trying new activities, and learning about new places. Your destination might be on the other side of the state, across the country, or around the world. Many people return to the same place repeatedly for each of their vacations. This offers a sense of familiarity and comfort, yet doesn't expose you to new experiences.

You may be surprised to discover that for the same price as your annual trip to Florida, you could travel to Europe by taking advantage of discounted travel packages and airfares offered online. Visit travel-related Websites such as Hotwire.com, Priceline.com, Orbitz.com, and Travelocity.com. Research various vacation destinations that will allow you to experience a new culture or way of life.

✗ Take an Alternate Route to and From Work Each Day

If there's more than one route you can take to and from work, utilize them. Try to put as much variation into your everyday activities as possible. As you explore a new route to work, look at what's around you—take in the different scenery.

✗ Eat at Different Restaurants for Lunch Everyday

Instead of returning to the same convenient restaurant to grab your lunch each and every day, and instead of ordering the same meal, try new restaurants and new foods on a regular basis. Just the act of altering your diet slightly by trying new foods could provide plenty of inspiration in terms of your creative thinking abilities.

If you tend to eat foods that aren't too healthy, try improving your diet. This too will keep you in a happier and healthier state of mind. For example, if you're able to lose a few pounds and you ultimately begin to feel better about yourself (in terms of your physical appearance), your overall confidence level will vastly improve. This additional confidence and pride in yourself will impact your ability to generate more creative ideas and to think more clearly. It'll also improve your self-esteem and help to alleviate the inherent fear many people have when asked to brainstorm in a group situation.

✗ Take Adult Education and Enrichment Classes

If you live in or near a city, chances are there's an adult education program or community college in your area. Sign up for classes at night or during the weekends. The classes you take could improve your professional skill set, but you could also participate in classes on subjects such as creative writing, painting, drawing, flower arranging, gardening, or crafts. You'll probably find many potential classes designed to teach you new skills or hobbies. Best of all, adult education programs are usually extremely inexpensive and require a minimal time commitment. Stay focused on your goal of expanding your experiences and learning new things, whether what you learn directly relates to your career or not.

✗ Ask Questions

One of the very best ways to learn new things is to ask questions. Whenever you're talking with someone in your personal or professional life, even a salesperson you encounter at the store, ask questions. Broaden your knowledge about whatever it is you're talking about with the other person. If you're not sure what to ask, stick with the basics—*who, what, where, when, why,* and *how*—then go from there. If you don't get the answers you need from the questions you're asking, rephrase the questions or broaden their scope.

✗ Look at Everyday Things From a Different Perspective

No matter what activity you're experiencing, try to look at that experience from a different perspective. For example, what is the person next to you thinking and feeling? What's going through that individual's mind while he or she is experiencing the same thing you are?

If you're looking at a piece of artwork or a photograph, think about what was going through the artist or photographer's mind when it was created.

If you're in a debate or argument with someone, take a moment to think about their side and consider the points they're making based on something besides your own usual way of thinking.

When you watch the news on television, consider watching a different station periodically in order to obtain a different perspective on current events. There are many things you can do throughout your day in terms of thinking about everyday activities and events slightly differently.

✗ Listen to Music and Daydream

Go to the music store, pick up five different CDs featuring artists you like or have never heard, then find someplace where you can relax, listen to your music and do nothing but daydream for 15, 30, 45, or 60 minutes without interruptions. Try to do this daily, or at least once or twice per week.

When you daydream, allow your mind to wonder aimlessly. This doesn't have to be a brainstorming session in which you're trying to generate specific ideas. Instead, reflect on your day, your life, a specific event, a person, or some creative project you plan to work on. Allow the music to drive your thoughts.

As you continue to engage in this activity, mix up your music selection regularly. Combine your favorites with different genres of music. Choose music that conveys different moods. Slow, instrumental ballads will put you in one frame of mind, while the latest pop or country song will put you in a totally different mind set when you daydream.

✗ Find a Creative Outlet for Yourself

Outside of your work, find something you really enjoy that will allow you to express your creativity and give that creativity a voice. Some ideas might include: creative writing, drawing, painting, pottery, gardening, home improvement, playing a musical instrument, sewing, knitting, or photography. Once you find something you enjoy and that allows you to express yourself (even if you choose not to share what you create with others), make time in your weekly schedule to engage in the activity.

✗ Play the "What If" Game With Things You Encounter

Throughout your day, challenge your mind by playing the "what if" game. The rules are simple. Take an ordinary object, activity, or anything else and then ask yourself, "What if...?" For example, if you're looking at a dog, think about what would happen if the dog had a longer nose ("What if the dog had a 12-inch long snout?"), had five legs ("What if the dog had five legs?"), were able to speak English ("What if the dog could speak English? What would it be saying?"). What would the ramifications be of your "what if" scenario? How would things be different? Improved upon?

Here are a few more "what if" questions to get you started. Remember, you can and should apply this to almost anything. Think about the ramifications and results of each "what if" scenario.

- What if I wore just a Speedo or bikini to work?

- What if I had to walk to work instead of drive?

- What if raindrops tasted like coffee?

- What if everyone in the world got along peacefully?

- What if there was no more disease?

- What if cars were fueled by water instead of gasoline?

- What if I graduated from college with a degree in marketing instead of accounting?

- What if I learned how to speak Spanish as well as English?

- What if I joined a dating service and met my soul mate?

- What if I quit smoking and began working out several times per week?

- What if the sky was green and grass was blue?

- What if I married my high school sweetheart instead of my current spouse?

- What if I was a multimillionaire?

- What if I was dirt poor and homeless?

- What if I colored my hair purple?

Change the Scenery

Sometimes, what we all need is some inspiration resulting from a change of scenery. If you live in the city, take a day trip out into the country and explore. Enjoy nature—the trees, fresh air, lakes, hiking trails, and wildlife. If you live in the country, take a day-trip into the city, then spend the day exploring, shopping, dealing with crowds, and going to the theater, opera, or ballet. Taking a day trip just once per month can give you a whole new perspective and change your mood as well as your mindset.

Creative Thinking Exercises

The activities and exercises you just read about were designed to help you broaden your horizons and have new inspirational experiences that you could later draw upon when generating ideas. This section offers a bunch of activities designed to force you to think creatively in a wide range of situations. When participating in these exercises, the idea is to actively use your creativity on a conscious level.

The following creative thinking exercises are described in no particular order. Choose the ones you're most comfortable with and give them a try, starting immediately. It's an excellent strategy to mix and match these activities as you work them into your schedule.

Consider each of these activities as practice sessions for tapping into your creativity. While most of them won't actually benefit you at work, they will help you enhance your creative thinking skills and can be highly enjoyable.

✎ Create a Personal Diary

Visit any bookstore and pick up a blank diary or journal with a cover and paper that inspires you. In your diary, start making daily entries and be sure to retell stories about your life experiences. Write about your daily activities, thoughts, desires, dreams, and whatever else you choose. Be as personal and intimate as you desire. Use this as a creative writing exercise that will also help you get to know yourself better.

✎ Create a Scrapbook or Photo Album

If you're like most people, you probably have a drawer or box filled with photos that were never organized or placed neatly in albums. Creating a personalized scrapbook or photo album can be a highly creative activity. To get started, visit any stationary store or craft shop and pick up some basic scrapbook supplies. If you're creating a photo album, visit a photography or camera shop to choose an album that inspires you. To begin tapping into your creative skills, start out small. Select a handful of 10 or 20 photos from a particular event in your life that holds fond memories and create a scrapbook or album that retells a story using those photos. Feel free to add captions or any other creative elements.

✎ Stare Up at the Clouds

Looking at the shapes of the clouds you see, use your mind's eye to create pictures, then make up stories in your head about what you see.

✗ Build Something with Legos

Go to your local toy store and buy yourself a Lego set. Use the Lego blocks to build a castle, an airplane, or anything else that comes to mind. Try to avoid following the directions. Instead, put the pieces together and see what you can create from scratch by yourself. Legos can actually be used to create art. One easy way to do this is to design a mosaic. According to the Lego Website, "the mosaic is a classic art form that has brought style and beauty to palaces, temples, and homes all throughout history. A mosaic is created by setting many small pieces into a flat pattern. Each piece is a single color and shape on its own, but when they are assembled together, a detailed picture appears." For more details, visit the Lego Website at *www.lego.com/mosaic*.

✗ Plant a Garden

When designing your garden, choose an assortment of colorful flowers, and create a design that you think will look attractive once the flowers start to bloom. Once the planting is done, add some garden ornaments to personalize your garden.

✗ Color in a Coloring Book With Crayons

If you're not comfortable drawing pictures freehand, buy a coloring book and use crayons to add color to the pictures. It's perfectly okay to regress back to childhood for this activity as you tap into your creativity and express yourself by coloring with crayons. To download free pages to color, visit the Nickelodeon Website at *www.nickjr.com/grownups/home/printables/blue/index.jhtml*.

✗ Redecorate a Room of Your Home

Set a predefined budget for yourself (it doesn't have to be too large) and use that money to redecorate one room of your home. Rearrange the furniture, replace the curtains, add new accessories, and paint the walls. Personalize the room using your creativity.

✗ Read a Children's Storybook

Whether you're alone or with kids, read the book *out loud* and make up funny voices for each the characters. Act out the book, don't just read it.

✗ Create Objects Using Clay, Play-Doh, or Silly Putty

Mold the compound with your hands. Create shapes, then transform those basic shapes into objects.

⚘ Write Poetry

Pick a topic, any topic, then write a poem about it. If you're not yet feeling creative enough to write a poem from scratch, get your hands on a Magnetic Poetry set. Each piece in a Magnetic Poetry set is a small magnet with a single word on it. Sets contain between 220 and 400 words. You can move the single word magnets around to create phrases, sentences, and full-length poems. Some Magnetic Poetry sets are based around themes, however, the Original Edition is perfect for the beginner. You can even play with some of the Magnetic Poetry sets for free, by visiting the Magnetic Poetry Website, *www.magneticpoetry.com*. Click on the "Play Online" icon. This is an easy, yet wonderfully creative activity. According to company founder Dave Kapell, Magnetic Poetry is used by professional songwriters, for example, to trigger ideas for lyrics. This is done by mixing

and matching seemingly unrelated words into sentences that actually make sense. "It's all about having our minds translate the chaos associated with seeing hundreds of random words spread out before us and trying to create order by linking words into phrases, sentences, and paragraphs. Creating order from chaos is a natural instinct and something the human mind does well. Being able to move the word magnets around will inspire ideas as your mind makes all sorts of connections and associations. If you start out with the goal of writing a love song or poem, you can use Magnetic Poetry to link random words together into sentences that have a romantic theme," explains Kapell.

⚘ Play a Computer Game That Encourages Creativity

Some computer games offer mindless entertainment and require nonstop shooting or twitch movements. Others, however, combine creativity and strategy, allowing you to tap into your creative thinking abilities to build and manage empires, cities, zoos, and theme parks, for example. Some of the best computer games for teens and adults that require creative thinking include:

- 🐾 SimCity 4 (Maxis-EA Games, *www.Simcity.com*).

- 🐾 The Sims and The Sims Online (EA Games, *http:// thesims.ea.com*).

- Age of Empires II (Microsoft Games, *www.AgeOfEmpires.com*).
- Rollercoaster Tycoon 2 (Infogrames, *www.rollercoastertycoon.com*).
- Empire Earth (Sierra, *www.EmpireEarth.com*).
- Zoo Tycoon (Microsoft Games, *www.ZooTycoon.com*).

These games are all about building, creating, and managing—not winning or losing. As a result, these games have unlimited playability. You take control and ownership of what you create during each simulation.

Play Chess or Another Strategy Game

You don't need a computer to play a game that requires strategy and that makes you think. Chess, checkers, backgammon, Scrabble, and Monopoly are all examples of games that can enhance your creative thinking abilities.

Doodle

Grab a pen and some paper and start doodling. Draw anything. You don't need any artistic ability to doodle. You can draw shapes, designs, characters, or objects. As you're doodling, make up stories in your head about what you're drawing. Start with a basic shape, like a circle or square, then turn it into something by adding details, such as a face, arms, and legs, for example.

Think up Different Uses for Ordinary Objects

Back in Chapter 1, you were asked to take an ordinary paper clip and come up with five different uses for it, besides holding a few sheets of paper together. Pick any other object and do the same exercise. Try this several times per day with different items, such as a pen, coin, rock, thumbtack, rubber band, or computer cable, for example.

Meet Someone New and Strike up a Conversion About an Unusual Topic

Not only will meeting someone new create a new experience for you and perhaps broaden your horizons, by selecting an unusual topic to discuss, you're mind will be forced to creatively hold up your half of the conversation.

Create a Personal Web Page

Even if you can't program a computer, there are free services you can use to create personal Web pages. Design a page that tells visitors all about you, your city, your favorite hobby, or anything else that's important to you. Create original text and incorporate photographs or other graphic images. Make full use of font styles, sizes, and colors. Without any programming, you can create a Web page for free (from any computer that's connected to the Internet) by visiting a service such as Yahoo Geocities (*www.Geocities.com*). Using America Online, use the keyword phrase "My Web Page" to create a personal Web page based around a wide range of themes.

✗ Bake Something from Scratch

Grab yourself a cookbook and bake something from scratch. Once you've baked a cake, cupcakes, or cookies, tap into your creative energies for decorating ideas. Use frosting and sprinkles, for example.

✗ Create a Photo Essay

Purchase a disposable camera or buy one role of film for your camera. Pick a topic and create your own photo essay by going out and taking pictures based on a theme, idea, or concept. For example, you could create a photo essay about your home, your city, the local zoo, a person, or anything else. Limit yourself to telling your story using fewer than 12 pictures. They say a picture is worth a thousand words. With 12 pictures, you should be able to tell a detailed story or convey an interesting message.

✗ Use Unusual Words in Sentences

Open a dictionary and randomly select a word you're not familiar with. Learn the definition of that word, then create five or 10 different sentences using that word. Force yourself to create sentences that are serious, are humorous, convey an emotion, or make a specific point.

Kick-Start Your Brainstorming Sessions

Creative thinking isn't something that most people can turn on and off on demand. Thus, when you (and a group of people) are engaged in a brainstorming session—with the goal of developing ideas to solve a specific problem, for example—it may be necessary to use some type of activity to get the creative process going. Typically, to develop new and exciting ideas, people need inspiration.

The following are a few activities that will get people's creativity flowing at the start of a brainstorming session or when, for whatever reason, the ideas aren't being generated. Like everything else, using these techniques will require practice and the cooperation of everyone in your brainstorming group. Be persistent and stay focused on the task at hand.

✗ Triggers

Pictures, objects, toys, or anything else can be used as a trigger. Use whatever is at hand, such as a photograph or item, and start making random associations between that item and your task at hand. Extract a concept or idea from the picture or item, then use this idea to stimulate a possible solution to your problem. Begin by trying to come up with the wackiest, most outrageous ideas first, based on whatever pops into your head.

✗ Random Words

Like triggers, random words can also inspire. Pick a few words at random and somehow connect them to the concept you're brainstorming about. Use the random words to make associations and link otherwise unrelated ideas or concepts together. The concept behind this strategy is that you will be forced to approach the thing your brainstorming about from a different angle. For a free random word brainstorming exercise, visit the Website *www.brainstorming.co.uk/onlinetools/websoftware.html*.

✗ Meditation/Visualization

This exercise involves sitting quietly in a comfortable environment, closing your eyes, relaxing, and then focusing on the problem at hand. Allow your mind to wonder. Play the "what if" game (see page 49) in your head. The key is to focus, but not think in an analytical way. You'll find that visualizing various scenarios in your mind's eye will help you be more creative and look at things from different perspectives.

✗ Ask Questions

Start with the basics (*who, what, where, when, why,* and *how*) then work your way toward asking all sorts of other questions that relate to the brainstorming objective at hand. Combine asking questions with the "what if" game, then add a touch of humor and outrageousness (nontraditional thinking), and you'll wind up generating ideas in no time.

✗ Mind Mapping

This brainstorming exercise was created in the 1960s by Tony Buzan and the Buzan Organization, Ltd. It involves combining words and visuals to layout ideas and concepts, then allowing your mind to expand upon those ideas and thoughts. It's an ideal tool for extracting information from your brain and then utilizing the information in a creative way. Mind Mapping can be done using a pad and pen, or with specialized software, such as Ygnius (*www.ygnius.com*) or Microsoft Visio (*www.microsoft.com/office/visio*). This technique can be done alone or in groups. Mind Maps allow you to show the structure of the key idea or concept, then the linkage between points and other concepts. This is a method for creative note taking that's ideal for working through problems, consolidating information, and presenting details in an organized way. Follow these directions for creating a simple Mind Map:

- Begin by writing the title (a keyword) in the center of a sheet of paper. Draw a circle around that word or phrase.

- For each subheading or ancillary concept, draw a line extending from the main idea (the circle in the center of the page), then write out the subhead. The nonlinear nature of Mind Maps makes it easy to link and cross-reference different elements of the map and associate key ideas.

- You can then draw lines extending from the subheadings. According to the Buzan Organization, Ltd., "When you have one idea but it seems to go nowhere, make it the centre of a mind map. The branches prompt you to add ideas at another level. A structure emerges. Soon that idea has become a whole concept. The Mind Map keeps all your ideas in front of you in a clear form. Each new idea is a centre of thought for more new ideas."

- Allow your thoughts to go out in many different directions from the main title on your Mind Map. Then create links between ideas. Be sure to stick with single words and short phrases.

- Add color to emphasis key ideas.

For complete step-by-step directions on how to create Mind Maps, point your Web browser to one of the following sites:

- *www.mind-map.com.*

- *www.mindtools.com.*

- *www.novamind.com/documentation/MindMapping.*

⁄ Storyboarding

Using a sheet of paper, draw four, six, or eight same-size boxes. Starting with the first box, draw or sketch pictures and incorporate words that will convey your idea or story. Storyboards are typically used by advertising executives when brainstorming and presenting ideas for TV ads, but you can create one for brainstorming ideas pertaining to anything that goes through stages. The pictures within your storyboard don't need to be detailed or works of fine art. Create simple sketches, line drawings, or stick figures that will help you generate and build upon ideas by seeing them graphically depicted on paper.

✗ Role-play

This exercise will help you see an issue from someone else's point of view. Take on the role of someone else, possibly a potential customer. Act how they would act, think how they would think. Use this mindset to approach whatever situation you're brainstorming about. Don't just think about someone else—become that person and act out scenarios either alone or with other people. If you're developing ideas for a new product, try taking on the role of the potential customer and consider things from their perspective, in terms of the design and functionality of the product, for example. As the customer, what would you want the product to offer, look like, feel like, etc.? Place yourself in the customer's shoes and become them.

All Play and No Work

There will be times when the best inspirations come from playing, utilizing toys, doing some type of arts and crafts, or watching TV—and *not* doing your traditional day-to-day work. As you're participating in these activities, you want to stay focused on the task at hand and try to avoid going too far astray.

If having fun, listening to music, or playing with toys generates the types of ideas you're looking for, then the time spent was productive and highly worthwhile because these fun activities inspired you. If, however, you're simply watching TV or goofing off, without generating the necessary ideas, you're not properly engaged in a brainstorming session or a creative thinking strategy. You need to reevaluate your approach.

While the various activities described within this chapter will help you to become a more creative thinker and help you to better tap into your creative energies when they're needed, there will be times when the ideas you need don't come to you. In these situations, you'll need to overcome "brainstormer's block," which is addressed in Chapter 5.

CHAPTER 5

Overcoming Brainstormer's Block

This book is all about enhancing your creativity, helping you generate bigger and better ideas, and determining how your thoughts can be transformed into positive results that will enhance your personal, professional, or financial life. By now, you should have a pretty good idea of how to tap into your creativity and address the situations in your life with new and innovative approaches that will lead you to success.

However, even the most creative thinkers sometimes hit roadblocks. Unfortunately, this is normal, so don't panic! For one reason or another, you may encounter times when your creative juices simply refuse to flow, or the outcomes you desire seem to be unattainable using your current approach. You know you're supposed to be thinking "outside of the box," yet you feel hopelessly locked within that box, with no escape in sight.

Hey, if those world famous magicians and illusionists can perform dramatic escapes from within a real-life locked box, you can certainly find your way out of an imaginary one with relative ease, especially once you know what's holding you back.

Chapters 3 and 4 introduced the concept of "brainstormer's block." This chapter will help you deal with those times when you experience it and can't seem to generate innovative, creative, and success-oriented ideas, or ultimately put them into action.

From this chapter, you'll discover:

- Easy ways to keep your creativity flowing on an ongoing basis.

- How to enhance those outside forces that truly inspire you.

- Strategies for pinpointing what's holding you back when you encounter brainstormer's block.

- Methods for overcoming creative blocks.

- Tips for dealing with tight deadlines and pressure to achieve quick results.

Earlier, you learned the importance of developing a defined goal or objective as you embark on a brainstorming session. If you begin to experience brainstormer's block, it's important never to lose sight of your initial goal or objective, but at the same time, determine exactly what's holding you back and why.

As you'll soon discover, by first understanding the specific situation you're in, the thoughts and emotions you're experiencing, and the physical or psychological obstacles that are currently in your path, your chances of overcoming your challenges increase dramatically.

In some cases, you may find that what's holding you back are some outside forces or circumstances that may or may not be beyond your control. In other situations, it may be your own insecurity or emotional state that's holding you back or creating the perception in your mind that you won't succeed in whatever it is you're setting out to accomplish. Step one to overcoming brainstormer's block is to determine what's holding you back and why. From there, you can address the situation and properly deal with it.

Keep Your Creativity Flowing on an Ongoing Basis

In your day-to-day life, being creative can be extremely beneficial, whether you're writing a term paper for school, creating a piece of artwork, writing a novel, writing business correspondence, putting together an important business presentation, or trying to come up with a new way to enhance productivity within your workplace. In other words, whatever it is you do, being a creative thinker can be extremely beneficial and help lead you to long-term success.

Even if you're not faced with a particular problem or challenge right now, don't let your mind stop working. Refrain from falling into a preset pattern in your life, in which you simply go through the motions without having to think. Not only will you be bored, but when the time comes when you need a creative idea or solution to a problem, your mind won't be as prepared to come to the rescue with a great idea, because it'll be out of practice. You can't run a marathon without proper training, practice, and preparation first. The same holds true for brainstorming.

There are many ways to tap into your creativity throughout the day. In the previous chapter, you read about activities and exercises you can implement in order to constantly improve your creativity and ability to brainstorm. Throughout the day, whether it's within your personal or professional life, it's important to develop some type of creative outlet for yourself that's enjoyable to you.

The idea is to challenge your mind and allow yourself a form of free expression. You might, for example, choose to:

- Complete crossword puzzles or try to solve brain teasers.

- Doodle or draw.

- Maintain a diary.

- Paint.

- Play a musical instrument and/or write music.

- Play chess, checkers, or another strategy-oriented game.

- Redecorate your home.

- Write poetry, a story, or a novel.

- Play tennis, basketball, football, or some other active sport that requires strategy.

Throughout your day, you probably embark on a wide range of activities, all of which take up time, energy, and resources. These activities also might have a cost associated with them. For every single activity (one at a time, of course), try to brainstorm throughout the day about ways each activity could take up less time, utilize less energy, require fewer resources, or how you can somehow cut the associated cost.

Simply by clustering similar activities together, such as your errands, or taking a more organized approach to completing them, you might be able to save an hour or more per day, thus making you more productive and giving you more time to do the things you enjoy.

Chances are, you won't be able to change every single aspect of your life, but by simply rethinking the way to do some everyday activities, at home, at work, or while on the go, you can brainstorm and implement ways for making your life better, less stressful, and more productive.

You'll discover that finding ways to use your brainpower throughout the day is easy, fun, and challenging—all at the same time. Yet, as you develop the ability to think creatively without making a conscious effort to do so, your ability to face more difficult or more meaningful challenges will become far easier.

Enhance the Outside Forces That Truly Inspire You

Inspiration is one of the keys to successful brainstorming. When you're trying to develop new, exciting, and innovative ideas, put them into use, and generate positive results, you need to be inspired. You need to plant the seeds in your head that cause your brain to generate the new ideas you're looking for.

Students, business people, homemakers, teachers, novelists, poets, painters, songwriters, musicians, and other creative people all get inspired by a wide range of things, such as events in their lives, things they witness, smells, tastes, sounds, or visuals. In the case of an artist, for example, something clicks in their mind that causes one event or experience to be transformed and developed into a form of expression that results in a new and original work of art. Chapters 10 and 11 offer practical advice and information from people from all walks of life who have mastered the art of brainstorming and creative thinking.

In addition to your own experiences and knowledge, the people around you can provide inspiration, as can dreams, desires, and goals. Allow the makings for ideas to come from anything and everything. However, as you do this, try to determine what in particular inspires you and helps you to be creative. Understanding how your own mind works will allow you to create the best possible environment for yourself when it comes time to participating in one of those all-important brainstorming sessions.

If, for example, you need to develop a creative and effective sales presentation in order to land an important account for your company, you could start from scratch and try to do everything yourself, or you could become inspired by those who have developed highly effective sales presentations before you. Try incorporating and improving upon some of their ideas and approaches instead of reinventing the wheel, so to speak. If possible, watch videos of previous presentations by other people. Perhaps seeing other successful people in action will inspire you to achieve similar results and to better tap into your own creativity. Don't be afraid to learn from other people and work toward making already established ideas even better.

Whenever you need to brainstorm, for whatever reason, create an environment for yourself that's conducive to generating the results you want and need. Everyone gets inspired by different things and works better in different environments, so it's important to get to know yourself and how your mind works best.

If you're more creative sitting alone in a room, with Mozart playing in the background and candles lit all around you as you think about a specific goal or objective, create that type of environment for yourself—or one that will allow you to relax and open your mind to creative thought. The more you do to make the brainstorming process easier for you personally, the better the results will be. Discover what inspires you and make sure those inspirations are present as you attempt to tap into your creativity in order to achieve a specific goal or objective during a brainstorming session.

Determine What's Holding You Back

These days, most people live stressful and hectic lives. We're all overworked, underpaid, and even less appreciated. Yet, we're expected to continue to meet or exceed deadlines, quotas, or productivity levels on an ongoing basis, while juggling our personal lives and all aspects of our professional lives at the same time. It's no wonder that, from time to time, you're not going to be in a particularly creative mood, even when you need to be.

People are less creative when they feel afraid, stressed out, hungry, tired, thirsty, pressured, overwhelmed, or when they're thinking about too many things at once and lacking focus on the issue(s) at hand. When and if you begin to experience brainstormer's block, it's important to determine what's keeping you from achieving success and what specifically can be done to put you in a better frame of mind.

Obviously, a two-week vacation on the beach in Hawaii or at a fancy spa is the ultimate cure for most people who feel overworked and stressed-out, yet it's important to be realistic at the same time. Face it, there are going to be times in your life when you're forced to deal with pressure, tight deadlines, and overbearing superiors breathing down your neck. Once you identify what these negative forces are, however, you'll be in a better position to understand and deal with them in a logical manner so that they don't hinder your ability to be creative and think clearly.

If you feel that your creativity and productivity are being hampered, invest the time to determine what the primary causes are (or might be). You may find that an event in your personal life, such as an argument with a spouse or child, is impacting your day on the job. Instead of allowing frustration with yourself or your situation to build up, thus making matters worse, create a list of what's on your mind or what's bothering you. Then for each item on that list, come up with several possible ways of fixing or improving that situation.

Ask yourself these questions:

- What's bothering me?
- What impact is it having on me?
- Why is this having a negative impact?
- How am I feeling emotionally?

🐾 How am I feeling physically?

🐾 What specific steps can be taken, starting immediately, to improve the situation?

As with everything else you do, try to take a well-thought-out and organized approach to fixing the situation and eliminating the brainstormer's block you're experiencing. If possible, don't rely on quick fixes or artificial cures. If you're feeling stressed out, don't immediately turn to a cigarette or a glass of wine to relax you. These efforts might temporarily mask the symptoms, but they won't fix the underlying problem.

Likewise, don't let a situation build up and get out of control. Being under a tight deadline is stressful enough. Don't deprive yourself of sleep or food, for example, which will only make a bad situation worse. Even if you're under a tight deadline, if you need a 10-minute break to take a walk, get fresh air, and clear your head, that is 10 minutes that will be well invested.

You won't ever simply experience brainstormer's block for no reason. If you contemplate the situation and examine it, you'll be able to determine the underlying cause and resolve the situation enough to get your creative juices flowing once again.

Overcoming Creative Blocks

Just as there are many potential causes for creative blocks, there are also countless fixes for them. In Chapter 3, you learned about different common methods for brainstorming. You also learned that there are no precise rules for brainstorming and that you should follow the procedures that work best for you.

If you have a clearly defined focus or objective, but one method of brainstorming isn't working for you at a particular time, try something different. Whatever you do, don't just stare at a blank sheet of paper and pressure yourself into coming up with great ideas—that won't work.

In addition to analyzing what might be blocking your creative flow, consider reworking or at the very least reevaluating your goal or objective for the brainstorming session. Perhaps it's too broad or vague and needs to be defined better. It's always a good strategy to start with the broadest possible objective and then narrow it down until it becomes exactly what you're hoping to achieve. From there, you'll better be able to generate the ideas you're looking for, by following the strategies outlined in Chapters 3, 6, and 7.

Becoming a creative thinker and expert brainstormer means learning how to look at things, such as problems, obstacles, or challenges, from many different perspectives and come up with potential solutions that aren't obvious, traditional, or straightforward. In other words, never create artificial blocks for yourself or write off bad ideas before they've been properly evaluated. What may at first appear to be a far-out, impractical, or outrageous idea may ultimately be modified into the ultimate solution you're looking for—the idea that generates the desired results.

As you embark on your brainstorming, don't limit yourself to just one brainstorming technique or idea-generation method. Try two or three different methods, or try revisiting ideas on different days when you're in a different mindset. Different brainstorming techniques are apt to generate different results. Only when you begin to analyze your results from a brainstorming session will you be able to determine what methods worked best when addressing a particular situation.

Likewise, one technique that's worked well for you in the past may not be the best approach for a totally different situation. For example, if you're trying to develop a new marketing campaign for a product your company is about to launch, using a traditional outlining method may not be the best approach for generating ideas, even if you consider yourself to be a skilled outline generator.

Finally, don't be afraid to walk away from a problem or brainstorming session, take some time to clear your head, and then return with a fresh perspective. There could come a time in any brainstorming session when you get burnt out. Give your mind a chance to focus on something else—something unrelated and, preferably, enjoyable—before returning to the task at hand.

Activities To Clear Your Mind

- Take a walk outside—get some fresh air.
- Go into a quiet room, close your eyes, and relax for a few minutes.
- Utilize deep breathing exercises, yoga, or chanting to center yourself.
- Call a friend or relative and focus your mind on something unrelated.
- Listen to music that puts you in a good mood.
- Participate in an activity you enjoy.
- Get something to eat or drink (avoid artificial methods of relaxation, such as alcohol, caffeine, or cigarettes, if possible).

For people who have experienced the positive results of mediation, yoga, deep breathing, stretching, chanting, or physical exercise as a way to clear their mind and relax, don't be afraid to utilize these activities when you experience brainstormer's block as a result of spending too much continuous time focusing on one thing.

When you're experiencing brainstorm's block, one of the worst things you can do is stop everything and sit around waiting for an idea to hit you. Instead of waiting around and doing nothing except agonizing over the fact you're not getting anything done, implement different brainstorming techniques and try to approach the problem or situation from a totally different perspective.

Deal Successfully With Tight Deadlines and Pressure

Unfortunately, you often can't eliminate deadlines, nor can you extend them. You have to properly manage your time in order to achieve everything that needs to be accomplished within a predetermined time period. In these situations, nothing replaces the implementation of good time management skills.

When you're confronted with a major task that must be completed in a predetermined amount of time, start off by developing a preplanned schedule for yourself and then sticking to that schedule. Follow these time-management strategies for dealing with deadlines:

1. Determine your ultimate objective and deadline.

2. Create a detailed to-do list of everything that needs to be done in order to achieve that objective. This is done by dividing the primary objective into smaller, more manageable objectives.

3. Take your written to-do list and put each item in order based on its priority or level of importance. Figure out what needs to get done and in what order. This will probably require totally reworking or reordering your list. If two items on the list need to be completed simultaneously, make note of this.

4. Select a start date for the project (keeping in mind that you already know your deadline for completion). Figure out exactly how much time you have to complete the overall objective.

5. For all of the items on your list, determine how long each will take to complete.

6. Using a calendar, day planner, or some type of scheduling software, plug in each item on your to-do list, creating a deadline by

which it must be accomplished, in order to ultimately achieve your final objective on time. As you schedule in each item, allow some leeway for unexpected events or delays that are outside of your control.

7. Anticipate all of the things that could conceivably go wrong as you're working toward your objective and develop a game plan in advance for dealing with those problems when and if they arise.

8. Once you've developed a realistic schedule, stick to it and stay focused. As each item on the list is completed, check it off and begin working on the next, always getting closer to achieving your ultimate objective.

While you can easily learn how to organize yourself better and manage your time better, you can't always get rid of the pressure and stress you experience each day. You can, however, learn how to channel that energy and make yourself more productive, as opposed to being too frazzled to think clearly.

How you deal with and work toward alleviating stress will have a huge impact on your overall health, happiness, productivity, and ability to enjoy your personal time. Unfortunately, there's no easy way to get rid of stress, but there are many things you can do to successfully manage it. Everyone deals with stress differently. The worst thing you can do for yourself is to accept the stress and do nothing to try to manage or control it.

If you have to deal with excessive levels of work-related stress, the first step is to carefully evaluate your professional life and pinpoint the exact causes of your stress. Next, consider consulting with your doctor or a stress management professional who can help you take control of the mental and physical impact of your stress. While you might feel better taking your frustrations out on your coworkers, clients, or family members by yelling at them or being nasty, this is never the best way to deal with stress.

Your diet, work patterns, mental discipline, and exercise habits all contribute to your ability to successfully manage stress. For example, simply by eliminating excessive sugar, processed grains, fats, and caffeine from your diet, most stress management experts agree that your body will be in better shape to help you deal with the physical impact of your stress.

Participating in an exercise program is another way to help yourself successfully control or alleviate the negative physical impact of stress. Your exercise can be working out at a gym after work and participating in an organized fitness program, such as aerobics, kick boxing, weight lifting, or jogging, or as simple as taking a walk around the block during your lunch break.

Throughout the day, take a minute or two to stand up, stretch, and take a few deep breaths. This is another fast and easy way to help control the physical impact of stress that your mind and body experiences.

If you know you're going into each project or situation totally prepared and approaching it in a well though-out and organized manner, you'll automatically feel less stress and pressure, because you'll know that everything is being done in the best possible way and that you're in control of the situation. When you're in this mindset, you'll find it much easier to think clearly, tap into your creativity, generate incredible ideas, implement those ideas, and ultimately achieve success.

CHAPTER 6

Analyzing Your Ideas

So, you've come up with a handful of ideas as a result of your brainstorming session. The next logical step is to scrap the ideas that are preposterous—the ones that have no shot of being widely accepted or that could not possibly help you achieve your goal. With those ideas off the table, it's time to take a look at what's left and do some careful evaluation in order to choose the best idea(s) to implement.

You already know that the time to analyze your ideas is *after* the brainstorming session, not *during* it. So once your brainstorming has come to an end, take a break. Allow your mind to focus on something totally unrelated. When you're ready to get back to work analyzing your ideas, you want to approach this process with a fresh perspective.

This chapter is all about choosing the best ideas, analyzing them, and deciding which ones are good enough to be implemented. Every time you reach this stage, how you analyze your ideas will be different, based on the situation at hand, the types of ideas you're evaluating, and what you want the ultimate outcome to be once you start the implementation phase. Your goal, however, is always to choose the best ideas. But, what constitutes an awesome idea, a good idea, and an awful idea? That's one of the things you're about to find out.

Ideas: the Good, the Bad, and the Ugly

It's been said that beauty is in the eye of the beholder. If you apply this wisdom to ideas, and consider a really good idea to be a beautiful thing, than there's a lot of personal objectivity involved when it comes to judging what a good idea really is.

If you're working alone and it's just up to you to choose the best idea and implement it, that can be challenging. After all, you want to make the right decision in order to insure success. In a corporate or group situation, where multiple people need to agree on an idea, as well as a method of implementation, the process potentially becomes even more complicated, because you're dealing with multiple points-of-view and opinions as to what constitutes a good idea to address a particular situation.

Once you have your handful of ideas, you need to establish the specific criteria by which each idea will be judged. To establish these criteria, a thorough understanding of the problem, as well as the desired outcome, is an absolute must (see Chapter 3). Before the brainstorming session started, you should have determined your problem, goal, opportunity, or objective, plus what you want the outcome to be. Go back and make sure this information is clear in your mind before trying to evaluate the ideas that were created during your brainstorming session.

Assuming you know your desired outcome, consider how the success of implementing the idea can be measured. Ask yourself:

✗ How would you describe a successful implementation of the idea? What specifically are you looking to achieve?

_____

_____

_____

_____

_____

✗ Specifically, how will the success be measured (qualitatively and quantitatively)?

_____

_____

_____

_____

_____

✔ Do you have enough background information and research data (if appropriate) to make an intelligent decision about which idea is the most feasible, based on the situation or problem at hand? If not, what additional information or data is needed before making a decision?

_____

_____

_____

_____

_____

_____

✔ What will be the criteria used to evaluate the success?

_____

_____

_____

_____

_____

✔ Who will be judging the outcome of the idea's implementation?

_____

_____

_____

_____

_____

✗ Ultimately, by what target audience will your idea be utilized? For example, if you're designing a new product, what is the target consumer group for the product?

_____

_____

_____

_____

_____

✗ Specifically what resources (manpower, budget, etc.) are available to help you implement your idea?

_____

_____

_____

_____

_____

✗ When will the ultimate success (or failure) of the idea's implementation be evaluated? What's your deadline to complete the implementation?

_____

_____

_____

_____

_____

Knowing this information, you can begin to weed our some of your ideas. Start by taking all of the ideas on your list and analyzing them one at a time. As you revisit each idea, in order to evaluate it, begin thinking analytically and realistically. Does the idea make sense financially? Can this idea really be implemented properly using the available resources and within the predetermined time frame?

Remember, there is no such thing as a bad, wrong, or stupid idea. Some ideas are usable, because they'll allow you to achieve your ultimate objective or solve a problem when they're implemented, and some ideas simply will not achieve this objective and can't be utilized. Don't automatically dismiss or reject any idea. Before tossing it, consider what positive aspects or potential the idea offers, even if the idea as a whole isn't suitable. Your ultimate solution may involve taking pieces of several ideas and somehow linking them together into one final idea.

As you think about each idea, ask yourself:

✗ How does the idea, if implemented properly, allow me to achieve the designated outcome or goal?

_____

_____

_____

_____

_____

✗ What is the allocated time available to implement the idea in order to meet the deadline? Is it possible to accomplish what needs to be done in the available time?

_____

_____

_____

_____

_____

✗ What resources will be needed, in order to successfully implement the idea? If the needed resources are not available, can they be gathered based on the financial and time limitations?

_____

_____

_____

_____

_____

✗ How feasible is the idea? How radical will people's current behaviors or beliefs have to change in order to successfully implement it?

_____

_____

_____

_____

_____

✗ How easy will it be to get others to accept the idea, make an emotional investment in it, and help achieve success? What will be required to do this?

_____

_____

_____

_____

_____

_____

✗ What are the positive aspects of the idea and the potential benefits or rewards associated with implementing it?

_____

_____

_____

_____

_____

✗ What are the potential drawbacks to the idea?

_____

_____

_____

_____

_____

✗ What are some of the possible difficulties or obstacles to be faced when implementing it?

_____

_____

_____

_____

One of the most important questions to ask about an idea is, does the idea you're analyzing give you that "Eureka!" or "Ah-ha!" feeling? Sometimes, you'll just know when an idea is perfect based on the feeling you get when you generate or analyze it. Your personal instincts are usually an excellent indicator, so trust them! The best ideas always have a personal passion behind them. Is this an idea that you totally believe in, 100 percent, and can easily get behind?

Next, for each idea, think about exactly how you'd implement it and what the overall short-term and long-term ramifications of the implementation will be on you, your company, and your customers (if applicable). Chapter 7 focuses on developing a detailed implementation plan for your idea. Until you finalize your decision about which idea you'll be implementing, think in more general terms about the feasibility of the implementation process in terms of cost, manpower, and resources that will be required. What basic steps will be involved in the implementation process?

Don't Just Rely on Your Own Opinions: Try a Focus Group

After a long brainstorming session, or when you're working under a tight deadline, it's possible to lose perspective. When a situation such as this occurs, you may convince yourself to adopt an idea, not necessarily because it's good, but because you're desperate. You become willing to make concessions and grab at any solution.

While it's always an excellent idea to go with your gut and trust your instincts, another excellent strategy for analyzing ideas is to bounce them off other people. Find people who were not involved in the brainstorming session and solicit honest feedback from outside parties.

You can hold a formal focus group or take a far more casual approach. A focus group involves gathering a group of people to see what they think about an idea. This can be done in person, online, over the telephone, or using written questionnaires.

There are many reasons to utilize a focus group in order to test out an idea. For example, a focus group could be used to gather a group of impartial people—not at all associated with the company or the generation of the idea—to provide honest and straightforward feedback about all aspects of a new product idea. These could be people from a different department within your company, friends who will be honest with you, random people off the street, or people who you identify as being your target audience.

For example, while a new product is still in the early concept phase, you could test out its feasibility on potential customers and get feedback about the product name, design, usage, ease of use, position in the marketplace, quality, packaging, performance, customer satisfaction, marketing, price point, consumer awareness, product testing, product comparison, and overall satisfaction.

A focus group can help you solicit other thoughts, opinions, and points of view you might not have already considered. According to Market Navigation, Inc. (*www.mnav.com/cligd.htm*), a market research firm based in Orangeburg, New York, focus groups are best used for:

- Exploration ("Fishing Expedition").

- Investigation (Detective Work).

- Identification of present practices.

- Understanding motivations.

- New idea generation.

- Communication refinement.

- Persuasion design labs.

- Strategic positioning.

- Word of mouth research.

The "Six Hats" Evaluation Technique

There are many techniques for evaluating new ideas. The "Six Hats" technique was developed by Edward DeBono (*www.edwdebono.com*), one of the world's leading authorities in the field of creative thinking and the teaching of thinking as a skill. It allows you to quickly evaluate almost any type of idea.

Using this technique, an idea is placed within a metaphorical (imaginary) colored hat and is tried on by the evaluator. Each colored hat represents a different mode of thinking, or an alternate point-of-view from which to evaluate an idea. For each idea you generate, try on each hat and see how it fits. Don't rely on just one hat to help you make an intelligent decision. Following is a summary of what each of the hats represents and how to think when wearing it. Remember that these different evaluations can be applied individually as well as in group situations.

Blue Hat   This hat is used to control the evaluation process and choose the best path to follow when analyzing your ideas. Ask yourself: What should be done next? How have I done so far? In what order should the hats be used?

Yellow Hat Use this hat to promote the power of positive thinking. Ask yourself: What are all of the reasons why the idea will work? What is good about this idea? What are the benefits? Who will benefit? How will the benefits happen? Is this idea right for the situation?

Red Hat   Think about your intuition, feelings, and emotions. Ask yourself: How do I feel about this? What intuition do I have? Your intuition doesn't need to be justified, but should be recognized as a factor in making intelligent decisions.

Black Hat This hat promotes judgment and caution (if needed), as well as a logical way of thinking. Ask yourself: What aspects of the idea will not work? What issues exist? Utilizing this hat when evaluating an idea will help keep you from making rash decisions and from doing insane things. The drawback, however, is that it's easy to over-evaluate or analyze something, so don't overuse it!

White Hat This hat represents the need for facts and figures, such as research data. Ask yourself: What additional information or research data is needed? What information is missing? How should I get the additional information that's needed? In terms of facts and figures, what's missing?

Green Hat This hat focuses on your creativity (lateral thinking) and encourages you to build upon the idea and expand upon it even further. Ask yourself: What new ideas do I have? What are the possibilities? What is the potential?

According to Edward DeBono's Web site, "The Six Hats method is a convenient and practical way to get the best out of individual and group thinking. It is a non-ego-threatening way to escape thinking ruts. It leads people away from considering only why things cannot work and guides them toward positive creative thinking. The thinker can focus on one mode of thinking (wear one Hat) at a time. Experience has shown that, once introduced, the Six Hats method has instant appeal and quickly becomes part of the corporate culture."

For more information about this idea evaluation technique, visit any of these Websites:

- *www.edwdebono.com/debono/video1.htm.*

- *http://members.ozemail.com.au/~caveman/Creative/Techniques/sixhats.htm.*

- *www.ronjonpublishing.com/powerpoint/ch16/sld030.htm.*

It All Comes Down to Making a Decision

The idea-evaluation process is the phase in the overall brainstorming process when a decision needs to be made. Keep in mind, you're not being forced to choose from the ideas you've already generated. It's acceptable to determine that your brainstorming session(s) didn't yet generate the idea(s) necessary to achieve the desired solution. As a result, additional brainstorming or research may be necessary. You're better off determining this now than investing the time, resources, manpower, and money into an idea that will fail because it didn't properly address the initial problem.

If you've done your research and have all of the information needed to make an intelligent decision, then chances are you'll know it when the right idea comes along. Of course, you will want to verify your gut feelings by evaluating the pros and cons of an idea and by determining how well the proposed idea addresses the issue at hand.

Another thing to consider is the pressure against change from the status quo that you might receive when implementing your new idea (either from within your company or from customers, for example). Also, after doing a purely financially based cost/benefit analysis, determine if the idea is feasible.

The Cost/Benefit Analysis Decision-Making Technique

A cost/benefit analysis is a purely analytical way to insure you won't be spending too much time, money, manpower, resources and/or energy on something that does not justify the expense. This type of analysis is relatively easy to do. Begin simply by adding up the value of the benefits resulting from the implementation of the idea, then subtract the costs associated with it.

For example, suppose you develop an idea for a new product. After sharing the idea with all divisions within your organization, you determine that the cost to bring that new product to market will be $5 million. This includes R&D, manufacturing, marketing, advertising, distribution, etc. Knowing your industry, the potential market, and your customer base, if your product's life-long sales are projected to generate only $4.5 million in revenue, than no matter how good of an idea for a new product you might have, from a purely financial standpoint, it isn't practical or feasible.

When doing a cost/benefit analysis, the data will usually be straightforward. There are, however, intangible costs or benefits that you won't easily be able to quantify with hard figures. For example, you might initially lose money on the launch of a new product, but by launching the product into the marketplace, you'll boost consumer awareness about your company and sales of your other products will increase. Something like the positive impact of a public relations campaign for a product, service, or company is also hard to measure quantitatively, even if it's highly successful.

The PMI Decision-Making Technique

Another simple decision-making technique is called PMI (Plus-Minus-Implications). Use it to weigh the pros and cons of an idea. To use this technique, on a blank sheet of paper, draw a table with three columns. The three column headings should be *Plus, Minus,* and *Implications*.

In the *Plus* column, make a list of all the potential positive results that you'll experience as a result of implementing your idea. Next, in the *Minus* column, write down all of the potentially negative things associated with the idea. Finally, in the *Implications* column, write down the positive and negative outcomes you're apt to experience by implementing your idea.

Once this is done, look at the *Plus* and *Minus* columns. Which list is longer? Chances are, a decision about whether or not to adopt the idea will become obvious. If not, take each item under each column and give it a point score from 1 (the most important or relevant) to 5 (the least important or relevant). Add up the scores for each column and see which one comes out the lowest. If the *Plus* column score is lower than the *Minus* column score, it is a good indication to move forward. The scores you award, however, can be highly subjective. You might want to get several opinions.

Create A PMI table like this one:

PLUS (Positive Outcomes and Benefits) with Related Score	MINUS (Negatives Aspects or Drawbacks) with Related Score	IMPLICATIONS

Total Score: **Total Score:**

_____   _____

As you can see, there are many ways to evaluate an idea. Choose evaluation and analysis methods you believe best apply to the type of situations you're dealing with. Based on your analysis, you should be able to take a handful of ideas generated during a brainstorming session and narrow them down to one or two really incredible ideas that you believe are worth implementing and pursing, in order to achieve success. Make educated decisions based upon known facts.

Later, in Chapters 9, 10, and 11, you'll be reading interviews with a handful of highly successful creative thinkers who share their advice about how they choose the ideas that they implement. These people have a proven track record for making the right decisions, so be open to learning from their experiences. In the next chapter, however, you'll read about strategies for actually implementing that awesome idea and making it a reality.

CHAPTER 7

Generating Tremendous Results From Your Big Ideas

This chapter is all about the implementation of your best ideas. It's about how you take that spark of brilliance that somehow popped into your head and transform it into reality so that you and/or your company can begin to experience positive results.

Depending on the type of idea you're trying to implement, this is the stage that determines your ultimate success and the level of difficulty you'll experience bringing your idea to fruition. This is the stage that requires total dedication, a true consensus within your organization, excitement, and the organizational skills needed to look at the entire picture and insure that all of the details are addressed.

In a corporate environment, idea implementation could easily be considered a form of project management. To make your ideas a reality, you and the people within your organization will need to rally behind the idea, utilize each of your specialties, work under deadlines, plus allocate the necessary time and resources. In some cases, once the creative aspects of the project are complete, implementation will require more traditional thinking and follow through.

The 10-Step Idea-Implementation Process

Because every idea is different and every organization is structured differently, there are no predefined rules for transforming an idea into reality. However, especially within an organization or business, there are a series of phases every idea must go through before it becomes a reality. For an individual working alone, because one person takes on many responsibilities and wears many hats, all of these phases remain important, but will most likely be handled differently than in a group.

This section will walk you through the general idea-implementation phases. Keep in mind, you may need to take additional steps or be able to skip certain steps, based on your idea and what your ultimate objectives are.

Step 1: Choosing the Best Idea

You've accomplished a lot if you've already pinpointed an objective, engaged in a successful brainstorming session, carefully analyzed each of the ideas generated during that session, and have ultimately selected the best idea that you now want to implement. Depending on what you're trying to accomplish, the next step—implementation—could be a very simply process, or it could temporarily turn your world upside down as you go against the established norm.

If you're working alone, choosing the best idea is somewhat easier, because you don't need approval or acceptance from a group. As long as you've properly tested and researched the idea and are convinced that the idea will lead to greater success if it's implemented correctly, then you have the power to make it happen.

In a group situation, once you think you've created the best possible idea to address a problem, situation, or goal, it's vitally important that the people within your group, department, team, or entire organization see your vision, agree with it, and totally believe that implementation of the idea will lead to success. Again, how widespread the acceptance of the idea needs to be depends on what the idea is and who it affects.

If you've generated an idea for a new television ad, for example, perhaps you only need acceptance and support from the top-level management and the people within the company's advertising or marketing department. If the idea is broader in scope and will somehow impact everyone within your organization, such as an idea for a new product, then the support of everyone will vastly improve your chances for a successful implementation of the idea.

Whatever you do, never move forward toward implementing an idea until you and the people with whom you're working are totally convinced that you have created and selected the best possible idea or solution for the situation at hand. If you're not 100 percent comfortable with the idea, go back to the brainstorming phase and rework the idea or come up with totally new ideas.

Make sure the idea you've selected has a really good chance of success once it is implemented. This should have been done after your initial brainstorming session(s), when you went back to analyze each idea and selected the best one. Once you're convinced you've generated the idea needed to achieve the solution you're seeking, the implementation phase of the entire brainstorming process can continue.

Step 2: Select a Project Leader

If you are working alone, you are by default, the project leader. It is your job to look at the big picture as the idea gets implemented. It is also your responsibility to handle all of the details and tasks needed to implement the idea.

In a group situation, one person should be assigned to be the project leader. This may or may not be the same person who served as brainstorming facilitator. This is the person who will oversee every detail of the implementation, maintain an understanding of the big picture, keep everything and everyone focused and organized, plus take charge of coordinating the details involved in the implementation process.

A project leader or project manager could be a top-level executive, department manager, team leader, or anyone else who has a thorough understanding of the objective (what you're trying to accomplish), the idea itself, and the process for accomplishing the objective. Ideally, this should be someone with experience overseeing and managing projects of any kind.

The project manager needs to be well organized, responsible, and able to motivate and manage people. Software packages, such as Microsoft Project 2002, can be helpful because they're ideal for managing projects involving many tasks, scheduling, resource allocation, and teams of people.

Step 3: Additional Research

Knowledge is power. Before moving forward, everyone needs to understand specifically why a new idea is being implemented. They should also know about the problem that's being addressed, and have a thorough understanding of the intended solution. As you proceed forward, it is important to make sure everyone involved is equipped with all of the pertinent information and research. If additional research needs to be done, now is the time to do it.

For example, you may decide to move forward with a new product idea and obtain favorable feedback from every division within the company (R&D, marketing, manufacturing, sales, etc.) As you move forward, however, the R&D department begins doing its job (not having done enough research beforehand) and determines that to develop and manufacture the new product, specialized equipment must be purchased, at a cost of $3 million. This was an unforeseen expense that could jeopardize the success of the overall idea implementation.

If you're a writer, for example, perhaps you've brainstormed an idea for a new book. You love the idea and become excited about the project. You invest significant time and effort in developing an outline and proposal to submit to publishers, only to determine there are four other virtually identical books already on the market. Through research, this waste of time and energy could easily have been avoided.

Depending on the types of ideas you're working with, creating a detailed business plan might be appropriate. A well-thought-out business plan will help you determine whether or not your idea is actually viable. The more details your business plan contains, the better your long-term chances for success will be.

The Anatomy of a Business Plan

Through the use of text, charts, spreadsheets, and graphics, a traditional business plan (or a similar document that outlines your strategies to implement an idea) will probably include most, if not all, of the following sections:

- The Company Name—the first line on the first page of any business plan.

- Executive Summary—provides an overview of the business.

- Objectives—describes what the goals of the business are or will be.

- Mission Statement—briefly expresses the company's overall purpose.

- Keys to Success—explains what your company will offer that will make it successful and what it will do differently.

- Risks—outlines the risks the company is going to face.

- Company Summary—provides more details about the company's products and/or services.

- Company Ownership—supplies information about the executives/founders involved with the company.

- Start-Up Summary (including financial projections)—explains what will be required to get your company launched.

- Start-Up Assets Needed—lists the assets your company needs prior to its launch.

- Investment—indicates where the initial start-up capital is coming from (loans, private investors, etc.).

- Company Locations and Facilities—tells where the company will be located and from what facilities it will operate.

- Detailed Product/Service Descriptions—explains, in detail, what the company will be offering.

- Competitive Comparison—describes key competitors.

- Sourcing—lists your company's main suppliers.

- Technology—explains how technology will be used as a tool within your company.

- Future Products/Services—indicates the specific and new types of products or services your company will launch in the future.

- Market Segmentation—explains how your company fits within its industry and whether it will cater to a specific market.

- Overall Industry Analysis—provides a brief description of the industry in which your company will do business.

- Market Analysis—describes the target customer/audience for your company's products or services.

- Marketing Strategy—conveys your company's marketing, promotions, advertising, and public relations plans.

- Sales Strategy—explains how your company will sell and distribute its products or services.

- Service and Support—indicates the type of service and support your company will offer.

- Strategic Alliances—states how your company will benefit from developing and implementing strategic alliances with other companies in order to achieve its goals.

- Organizational Structure of the Company—describes the hierarchy of your company from the founder/president/CEO down to the entry-level people and outlines projected salaries.

- Financial Plan—contains detailed financial statements and projections.

To help format your business plan and compile the information you'll need, the Small Business Association's Website (*www.sba.gov/shareware/ starfile.html*) offers several free software programs designed to assist in the creation of a business plan using any desktop computer.

There are also a variety of commercially available, off-the-shelf software packages designed to assist in the creation of business plans, such as Palo Alto Software Products's Business Plan Pro 2003 and Business Plan Premier 2003 (1-888-PLAN-PRO, *www.paloaltosoftware.com*). These are easy to use, Windows-based business plan packages that feature context-sensitive audio help, more than 400 sample business plans, a large database of venture capitalists and information, customizable business charts, and the ability to generate professional-looking printouts. The plan wizard feature walks users through the business plan creation process, and allows for the full customization of a plan to fit any needs.

Step 4: Dissecting the Idea—Determining What Needs to Be Done

Because every idea is different and every organization works differently, no two ideas can be implemented in the same way. Thus, for every idea you choose to implement, it becomes important to dissect the idea and then figure out everything that needs to be achieved in order to implement it.

Ask questions such as:

- What specific steps need to be taken to implement the idea?
- Who needs to be involved in the implementation (in terms of departments, teams, and individuals)?
- Will outside specialists need to be brought in? If so, what types of specialists are required?
- What internal resources will be needed to implement the idea?
- What external resources must be acquired and in what time frame?
- How will implementing the idea alter day-to-day operations in the short run and long run? What past thought patterns will be changed or broken?
- What departments within the organization will be impacted by the idea's implementation?
- What are the costs associated with implementing the idea?

Pre-planning as much as possible and anticipating potential obstacles (and how to deal with them) will make the implementation process smoother, plus increase your chances for success.

Step 5: Rallying the Team or Organization to Get Totally Behind the Idea

Chances are, the person who generated the idea that you're thinking about implementing will already be extremely excited about it. Now your objective is to win over the enthusiasm and support of everyone else who will somehow be involved with the idea's implementation. You need to rally the troops and get everyone working toward a specific goal that they understand and are excited about. Make sure everyone understands the potential benefits and rewards if the idea is implemented successfully. Whenever possible, give people a personal stake in the success.

One of the best ways to rally people together is to demonstrate your own enthusiasm. You can also give people partial ownership of the idea if you encourage them to build upon it and improve upon the entire idea or the various steps that need to be taken to implement it.

If everyone is working toward a common goal, your chances of success improve greatly. While this concept applies to businesses, it also usually applies to individuals working alone, because no project is ever just a one-person endeavor. For example, the author of a book needs to sell his/her idea to a publisher. The people within that publishing company now need to be excited enough about the project to sell it to bookstores (to build a distribution channel), as well as to book reviewers and the media. Ultimately, the consumers need to become excited about it so they'll buy a copy of the book and read it.

Step 6: Developing an Implementation Strategy

There are specific strategies to incorporate when trying to achieve any goal. Once you know what you want the outcome to be, divide up that large goal into a series of smaller, more achievable "sub-goals," all of which will lead up to the primary goal's achievement.

Now that you know the specific steps that need to be taken to achieve the goal of implementing the idea, create a timeline for achieving each step. Determine the order in which the steps need to be completed. Also set deadlines for yourself and the people with whom you're working. Proper scheduling, plus personnel, resource, and cost management are all critical elements when managing any project.

Assign various people in your organization to individual tasks. Make them responsible for completing or achieving specific sub-goals. Remember, if all of the sub-goals aren't properly achieved, you will not achieve your ultimate goal. A breakdown in organization or communication, poor scheduling, or assigning unqualified people to specific tasks could all lead to delays, cost overruns, or ultimate failure. The implementation strategy you create should be well thought out, preplanned, widely accepted within the organization, and well documented. Now is not the time to be taking shortcuts to save time, save money, or to avoid paying attention to the details.

Step 7: Utilizing the Specialists and Resources Within Your Organization

Sometimes, it will come down to finding the best person for the job if you want to improve your chances for achieving success through the implementation of an idea. Once you know what needs to be accomplished and what skills or knowledge is required for each phase of the implementation process, assign the proper people to each task. If necessary, hire consultants or outside specialists. You may need to restructure your existing organization to better utilize the manpower at your disposal.

When you assign a task to someone, provide them with the background information that is needed, then give them ownership and responsibility as it relates to their specific task. Have the project manager keep tabs on each person, team, or department to insure progress is being made, but allow each person some autonomy to use their own creative thinking, skills, and experience to achieve their objectives.

Step 8: Setting Your Timeline

In some situations, delays are inevitable. Yet, if you preplan and schedule properly, you can eliminate many potential problems in advance. When working in a group situation, everyone needs to stay on schedule, especially when specific tasks need to be accomplished in a specific order. If one person or group falls behind, the whole project could suffer. Thus, multiple deadlines, all leading up to the final deadline, should be established. This applies if you're working alone or within an organization.

Once deadlines are established, make sure everyone is aware of them and understands why they're in place. If you can distribute a printout that graphically displays the timeline for your idea implementation, with deadlines clearly indicated, it could be a helpful tool. Software packages, such as ACT! 6.0, Microsoft Outlook, or Microsoft Project will allow you to create these customized printouts for each person involved in the project.

Creating a timeline that everyone can understand is as easy as drawing a straight (horizontal) line across a sheet of paper. At one end of the line, write today's date. On the opposite end, write in the final completion date. Now, on your timeline, mark each major task that needs to be accomplished, along with a corresponding deadline for that task. Use a timeline to help you stay organized and understand deadlines.

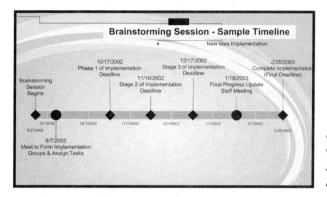

Sample Timeline Created Using Microsoft Visio Standard

To create organizational flowcharts and diagrams for showcasing timelines or tasks associated with the implementation of an idea, Microsoft Visio Standard 2002 (*www.microsoft.com/office/visio*) is a Windows-based software package that provides diagramming solutions to help people document and share ideas and information visually.

Diagrams created in Visio Standard provide valuable insights into existing processes, people, and projects, as well as help individuals and teams work together more effectively. When used to augment text and numbers, Visio diagrams make a message more concise and help people remember main points, such as deadlines.

Using Visio Standard, you can assemble diagrams using predefined shapes. There's no need to know how to draw. This allows you to add a professional look to your diagrams with just a few mouse clicks, then share your work in the context of your everyday business communications. Visio can be used to create flowcharts, organization charts, timelines, office layouts, and more. You can also generate diagrams from data stored in Microsoft Excel, Microsoft Access, and Microsoft Project.

According to Microsoft, "At the beginning of project planning, it's a good idea to gather project team members together to brainstorm and agree on major tasks and milestones. The perfect tool for capturing and communicating project milestones is a Visio timeline. A timeline is a horizontal line that represents the life of a project. By adding markers to the timeline, you can indicate project phases and milestones." For detailed instructions for creating a graphical timeline using Visio, point your Web browser to *http://office.microsoft.com/assistance/2002/articles/vspotlight2_nov00.aspx*.

Why is a timeline important? Well, if you need to launch a product in time for the Christmas shopping season, for example, you need to insure that each phase of your idea implementation (that is, the product design, R&D, manufacturing, marketing, advertising, public relations, sales, distribution, etc.) all work toward the deadline of getting the final product on retailers' shelves by a specific street date.

As the project leader, requesting periodic updates from teams or individuals is often appropriate. Creating an environment for achieving success could mean allocating additional manpower or resources to one stage of the idea implementation if something is falling behind. This would be at the discretion of the project leader or at the request of the person or team that is behind schedule.

You want to entrust people to take responsibility and do their jobs. If everyone is motivated and excited about the project, you'll find people will work extra hard to achieve their assigned objectives. Because some people freeze under pressure, make sure the deadlines are known, but don't harass people with constant reminders. When possible, try to use humor to motivate people. Threats, for example, create additional unwanted pressure. Later in this book, Jim McCann, the Founder and CEO of 1-800-Flowers.com, talks about how he uses humor to keep people motivated and on track during the implementation phase of a new idea.

Step 9: Putting the Idea Into Motion

After you've determined everything that needs to be done and have assigned specific people to handle various tasks associated with the implementation of the idea, it's time to let people do their jobs and put things into motion. As this happens, be on the lookout for obstacles and unexpected challenges, glitches, or situations that need to be addressed. When something arises, deal with it immediately, and adopt a creative approach to the solution, if necessary.

If you've done things correctly, the implementation of your new idea will change the way things have been thought about in the past, hopefully improving upon things. The new idea, once implemented, will open up a wide range of new opportunities and possibilities that will require additional brainstorming and creative thinking. This is a never-ending process. The implementation of new ideas will lead to the need or desire for even newer ideas or improvements.

Step 10: Examining the Results (Short-Term and Long-Term)

From the time you first identified a need, issue, situation, opportunity, or problem (your reason for brainstorming) to the time you've implemented one or more of the new ideas you generated, the length of time could be anywhere from a matter of minutes to several years or more, depending on the idea or situation. Companies especially tend to adopt more radical ideas quickly when they're desperate and traditional methods for doing things stop working. Individuals are more apt to adopt new ideas into their personal, professional, and financial lives if they see a clear benefit.

If you remember, the very first stage in the whole process is identifying the reason to brainstorm and determining what you want the final outcome to be. Knowing what you want or need as a final result, you can more easily measure the success of your idea implementation at every step along the way.

Early on, before you actually implement an idea:

- Establish the desired outcome. This should be clearly and specifically spelled out, with no grey area for later interpretation.

- Know how you will define "success" for the idea's implementation, by taking a practical and realistic approach.

- Determine how you will measure the results of your success. What criteria will be used and when?

- Decide who is responsible for measuring the results and making the proper interpretations.

Knowing this information will help you determine when you've achieved success and the results you desire. As an idea is being implemented, ask yourself:

- Is the idea that's been implemented generating the expected or required results?

- If expectations or projections aren't being achieved, why not? What has gone wrong? What needs to be modified or reworked? (Answering this question may require another brainstorming session.)

- What isn't being done yet that will allow you to achieve your objective or desired outcome?

- If the idea you've implemented has failed, should you rework it or start from scratch with an entirely new idea or approach? Have you given the newly implemented idea enough time to generate the desired results? (Your answers to these questions will be based on each unique situation, as well as on the time, resources, and new ideas that are available.)

Generating the Tremendous Results You Want

The idea implementation phases described in this chapter apply primarily to those big ideas that will be utilized within large companies or organizations. For example, all of these phases apply when launching new products or drastically altering everyday business practices.

For less grandiose ideas, some, but not all of these steps might be utilized. Instead of developing a full business plan, you might only need to create a one-page summary of the implementation strategy. Instead of bringing in a large group of people to help implement the idea, it might be something you can do alone or with a partner.

No matter what, your chances for achieving success are far greater if you are passionate about the new idea, do your research and preplan properly. Now that you have a good idea, and know how your new ideas will be implemented, in the next chapter you'll learn about specific brainstorming and implementation tools and products designed to make the whole process easier.

CHAPTER 8

Brainstorming Tools

Construction workers use hammers, screwdrivers, saws, and other tools to build. Artists use paints, brushes, and canvas. Musicians use musical instruments to create. As a creative thinker about to embark on a brainstorming session, you too can equip yourself with a variety of tools.

No matter who you are, or what you do, the single most powerful tool you have for brainstorming is, of course, your brain. To enhance your brainstorming ability and help you truly tap into the power of your brain, you will find it useful to utilize one or more tools. At the very least, you'll want to devise a method for documenting and keeping track of your ideas so you have a chance to later evaluate and possibly implement them.

Throughout this book, various brainstorming strategies and tools have been mentioned already. In this chapter, you'll learn more about specific low-tech and high-tech tools you can use to become a more creative thinker and more effective brainstormer. Whether or not you incorporate any of these tools is a matter of personal preference.

Low-Tech Tools

You'll discover later in this chapter that there are a wide range of high-tech tools, such as software packages, that can assist you in all aspects of idea generation and brainstorming. These tools can also help you take an organized approach to implementing your best ideas. In this section, however, we'll focus on more traditional tools that don't require a computer or technology.

You may discover that you work best combining both low-tech and high-tech tools when you brainstorm or need to tap into your creativity to solve problems and deal with various challenges.

Pad and Pen

Once you add creative thinking and brainstorming to your personal skill set, you should start keeping a pad and pen (or other writing instrument) nearby at all times. Carry a small notepad and pen in your pocket or purse. Keep a pad and pen on your desk, next to your bed, and in your car. You never know when an incredible idea will pop into your head—an idea that you'll want to write down so it's not forgotten.

Once you get into the habit of brainstorming and creative thinking, you'll find that some great (and some not so great) ideas will start popping into your head when you least expect them. Having the ability to instantly write down or sketch out your ideas is important.

There have been many stories from the world's greatest entrepreneurs and inventors that their greatest ideas came to them in the strangest places, like while eating at their favorite diner, during a drive, at the movies, or while playing a game of golf. You never know where your next inspiration will come from, so be prepared!

When an idea pops into to your head, even if it's in the middle of the night, write it down immediately. Once it's written down, go back to your previous activity, then revisit the idea at a more convenient time. Now that there's a written record, you don't have to worry about forgetting it.

Make it a habit to carry around a pen and paper with you at all times. Depending on how you spend your time and your personal preferences, you can purchase writing instruments that are waterproof, have a built in light (for writing in the dark), or that have multiple ink colors built into a single pen, for example. Some people prefer to brainstorm by writing their notes using an expensive pen from Mont Blanc. Others prefer the low cost and disposability of a Bic ballpoint, for example. It's true, some people get more inspired when taking notes or writing with a very specific type of writing instrument.

As for your paper, it's best to use a bound pad of paper, such as an inexpensive notebook, binder, or memo pad, (as opposed to loose scrap papers) in order to keep your thoughts safe and more organized. A bound diary or journal (available at bookstores) containing blank pages is also a useful brainstorming tool. Writing on random scrap papers won't help you take an organized approach to your brainstorming.

Whether you choose to write in pencil, ballpoint pen, rollerball pen, fountain pen, or even crayon, make sure that you have something nearby to write with and to write on. Don't be afraid to utilize these tools when the next big idea enters your mind.

Sketchpad

Some people brainstorm best using words and text. Others, who are more artistic, prefer to doodle or sketch out their ideas. Even if you're not a talented artist, a sketchpad allows you to artistically communicate and document your ideas using words, pictures, diagrams, and other visuals that you draw. For creative thinkers, sometimes a shape or design, as opposed to text, will trigger a thought process that leads to awesome ideas. As you tap into your creativity, don't be afraid to document your graphic ideas and inspirations.

When advertising executives are creating TV commercials, for example, they'll typically sketch out their ideas using a storyboard format in order to convey their "story" for the commercial graphically.

Tape Recorder

Do you sometimes think faster than you can write or type? Are there times when a great idea hits you, but you're driving a car or for some reason can't write down what you're thinking? In these situations, use a tape recorder and start talking—or singing.

These days, you can purchase a microcassette recorder that's smaller than a pack of cigarettes and a digital recorder (that uses no tapes) that's smaller than a ball point pen. Some digital recorders allow you to record several hour's worth of information. For less than $50, you can invest in a microcassette or digital recorder. Microcassettes are useful because they're inexpensive, small (about the size of a half-dollar), and will store your audio information permanently (or until the tape is erased).

Not everyone is comfortable talking into a tape recorder and later hearing their own voice. If you choose this method to save your ideas and inspirations, make sure you carefully mark all of your tapes so that you don't accidentally erase something important. Once you've saved something to tape, you can later go back and transcribe your recordings or play them back during your next brainstorming session.

The great thing about using a tape recorder is that you can speak, babble, sing, or record whatever sounds are around you. This is an easy thing to do when you're driving, for example. These devices are also excellent for keeping records during group brainstorming sessions.

Microcassette and digital recorders are sold at office supply superstores (such as OfficeMax or Staples) and electronics stores (like Best Buy or Radio Shack).

Camera/Video Recorder

Sometimes you can develop an idea that would take pages upon pages of text to communicate, or you could simply snap a picture of something that inspires you. Whether you prefer shooting still photographs or video images, there are small, lightweight, and inexpensive cameras available that you can carry with you.

For brainstorming, taking photos with a digital camera or Polaroid instant camera can make the process easier, because images can immediately be seen. There's no processing or wait time. With a digital camera, you can transfer your images to a computer, crop or edit them, and print them out for later reference. Some of the latest laptop computers, PDAs, and cellular phones now have built in digital cameras, so you can photograph things that inspire you wherever you happen to be.

For under $10, you can also purchase a disposable camera to keep in your car, briefcase, or purse. You don't have to be a professional photographer or even artistic to be able to take photos of things that spark your creativity or help you conceive of an idea.

File Cards

If you're not technologically savvy, yet you want flexibility to generate ideas or lists, move your thoughts around, or modify them and change their order, file or index cards are an ideal tool.

For each unique item, thought, concept, or idea, write it on a single index card. You can later lay out the cards on a table, rearrange their order, throw away cards, add cards, and then file your cards for safe keeping. You can also color-code cards, alphabetize them, or come up with your own system for managing the ideas you write on them. Out of all the brainstorming tools described in this chapter, index cards are one of the cheapest and most flexible in terms of their use.

Bulletin Board

You've probably seen this process used by detectives on television police dramas. Depending on the type of brainstorming you're doing, a bulletin board (corkboard) can be a useful tool. On the board, attach file cards, photos, diagrams, newspaper/magazine clippings, and other items that relate to your activities, creating a collage of words and images. You can then rearrange these items, add more items, and discard unwanted items as you formulate new ideas using what's on the board for inspiration and guidance.

You can use various software applications for the same purpose. However, if you're working with a group of people (in the same room) to brainstorm, utilizing a large bulletin board makes it easy for everyone to see the visuals involved in the idea-generation process. In addition to what's posted on the bulletin board, make sure everyone in the brainstorming session is also equipped with a pad and pen and is encouraged to voice their own ideas throughout the process. At the end of each brainstorming session, make sure a written or recorded record of what's on the bulletin board is created, so no ideas are forgotten.

Dry Erase Board/Whiteboard

Using a series of colored markers, a large dry erase board (white board) can be used for a variety of purposes, especially if you're working as part of a brainstorming group. On the board, you can list ideas, keywords, phrases, diagrams, drawings, and other visual images that can be color-coded. As new ideas or concepts are developed, others can be quickly erased. A dry erase board is an excellent tool for use during the initial idea-generation process. Alternatives include traditional chalkboards and large, presentation-size flip-chart pads that can be displayed on an easel and written on with markers.

High-Tech Tools

Computers are powerful tools and can be used for an endless array of specialized and complex applications. While scientists and programmers are striving to develop a true form of artificial intelligence that would allow a computer to think like a human and maybe even have emotions, right now, creativity and brainstorming are things you'll have to rely on your own brain to handle.

As you're about to learn, however, there is a wide range of different software applications that can be used to help facilitate brainstorming sessions when you're working alone or in groups. All of the computer applications described in this section is supported by the Microsoft Windows operating system.

You've already discovered that there are many ways of brainstorming, yet once you get started, it's important to keep the ideas flowing and to record those ideas for later evaluation. The software packages described here can help you collect and organize vast amounts of information, collaborate with others through rapid and real-time exchange of ideas, or assist you in your own brainstorming activities.

Keep in mind that these software packages are tools designed to make the busy work associated with brainstorming easier. None of these programs will replace the need for you to tap into your own creativity, generate ideas, define problems, or develop innovative solutions to those problems or challenges.

Because everyone has his or her own personal preferences in terms of the tools used to help inspire them, it's an excellent idea to utilize the free demo programs offered by many of these companies. The free downloadable demos will allow you to try the software firsthand to see if it's capable of handling the tasks you need to make your own style of brainstorming more effective.

The following are just a few of the many brainstorming, idea-generation, outlining, and rational database software packages on the market. Using any search engine (such as Yahoo.com or Google.com), use a search phrase, such as "outlining software" or "brainstorming" to find additional software products you might find useful. The prices provided throughout this section are current as of this writing, but may vary and are subject to change.

ThoughtPath Software

Company: Inventive Logic/Synectecs, Inc.

Phone: 1-617-869-6530

Website: *www.ThoughtPath.com*

Price: $99 (download edition), $125 (physical copy)

Th🞉ughtPath

Most database software packages will help you gather, manage, and share data. Inventive Logic's ThoughtPath, however, is a totally different type of computer-based tool. Utilizing more than 40 years of research by Synectics, Inc. (1-617-868-6530, *www.syntecsworld.com*), ThoughtPath offers a single person or a small group a powerful tool for actually enhancing creativity and generating ideas.

The software uses a proven methodology and several different "connection-making" exercises that allow people to take their brainstorming efforts to a higher level. In addition to helping to spur the creativity process, the software also tracks ideas in a built-in relational database, which can be searched using keywords.

According to Inventive Logic, which developed the software, ThoughtPath has been used highly effectively as a tool for facilitating small meetings and brainstorming sessions. It has been used by both individuals and companies for brainstorming that relates to product and service development, marketing and sales strategies, business and strategic planning, creative writing, career planning, and problem solving.

In addition to helping users generate ideas, ThoughtPath will also help evaluate and refine those ideas, and then generate customized reports that will structure your ideas and solutions for in-depth analysis or presentation to others.

The software's developer reported that "ThoughtPath is designed for creative problem solving and brainstorming. Once a problem has been defined, the software will help you to take a systematic approach to thinking about the problem and coming up with new and innovative solutions." The software is easy-to-use and requires little computer knowledge to operate. This is a powerful tool designed for people who need to think, want to be creative, and strive to be innovative in their ideas.

The software is divided into six primary modules, which Inventive Logic describes in the following way:

1. **The Gym**: A mental workout that includes a series of self-paced exercises and activities designed to enhance creativity. These activities focus on the use of triggers and creative thinking. For example, you may be asked for several unique ways to use a thimble, then be asked to list several situations in which you absolutely could not use a thimble for anything.

2. **Idea Generation**: Used for brainstorming new ideas from scratch.

3. **Guided Problem Solving**: A guided, step-by-step method for solving problems and developing innovative solutions.

4. **Problem Solving**: Use this module for more freeform and personalized problem solving.

5. **Evaluate and Refine Concept**: This module helps users evaluate and develop ideas not created using this software.

6. **Thought Warehouse**: This database can be used for leveraging your thinking across multiple problems using keywords and phrases.

Users experience exercises to help generate new ideas using what Inventive Logic calls "Excursion" and "Trigger" technology. Tools are then provided to mold almost any idea into a workable solution (using an "Itemized Response" process).

Jeff Mauzy, a principal at Synectics, Inc. and one of the primary developers of ThoughtPath explained, "Over the years, we've heard stories that our software has been used to generate ideas for new products, create the concepts for inventions, develop enhancements to existing products, and even for creating the plot for the motion picture *Ace Ventura II*."

He added that when someone decides to utilize the software, the first step is to be patient. "Use the software for the first few times when you're not in a hurry or under stress. Also, don't settle for the first few ideas you generate using triggers, for example. Keep going and dig deeper. This will give you a much larger array of ideas to ultimately choose from. Using the software, you have nothing to be afraid of. There's nobody to put down any of your ideas. One of the nice things about the software is that you don't have to present your ideas in front of other people. The software will never call you stupid, it doesn't care how long you take, and it doesn't care whether or not you can spell. Use the freedom that this software gives you to open your mind and allow your ideas to flow."

While it does not feature a lot of flashy graphics or a slick user interface, ThoughtPath is a unique tool that will help virtually anyone learn to be a more creative and innovative thinker. Perhaps this is why over the past 10 years, ThoughtPath has been put to use by thousands of business professionals working for companies in all industries. The software is available in the PC format and works on Macs running Windows emulation software and is probably the best software currently on the market for brainstorming and problem solving. For anyone who needs or wants to be creative, but needs a helping hand as they develop their brainstorming skills, this software is ideal.

(Portions of the preceding description were quoted and paraphrased from www.ThoughtPath.com.)

Inspiration 7

Company: Inspiration Software, Inc.

Phone: 1-800-877-4292

Website: *www.inspiration.com*

Price: $69

Originally designed for students, this software package can be used by anyone looking to energize their brainstorming process. Powered by the proven techniques of visual learning, Inspiration 7 is a computer-based tool for developing ideas and promoting organized thinking. Inspiration Software's integrated diagramming and outlining environments work together to help users better comprehend concepts and information.

Using the Diagram View module, users can create and manipulate concept maps, webs, and other graphical organizers. In this mode, ideas can be captured as quickly as someone thinks of them with the "Rapid Fire" tool.

With the integrated "Outline View," Inspiration Software's Website reports that "users instantly transform their thoughts into the foundation of written projects. The result is clearer thinking, more creative projects, better-organized writing, and improved performance. With the simple click of the mouse, users can transform a diagram into a traditional hierarchical outline. Using the 'Outline View' feature, it's easy to prioritize and rearrange ideas."

Because this software is designed for young people, virtually all of Inspiration's main functions are at your fingertips using the toolbars found at the top of the screen. There's no need to memorize keyboard shortcuts or search through menu items to find features.

Like ThoughtPath, Inspiration is an excellent tool for anyone to use during the creative brainstorming process. It is designed, however, for a single user—not a group brainstorming session.

(Portions of the preceding description were quoted and paraphrased from www.inspiration.com.*)*

Microsoft Project 2002

Company: Microsoft Corporation

Phone: 1-888-218-5617

Website: *www.microsoft.com/office/project*

Price: $599 (Standard Version)
            $999 (Professional Version)

One of the benefits of using Microsoft Project 2002 is that it's designed to seamlessly integrate with all of the other Microsoft Office XP applications, including Word, Excel, Outlook, and PowerPoint. Thus, data can be transferred between applications quickly and easily. Likewise, the user interface of this software is consistent with other Office applications, so if you're familiar with how Office works, the learning curve will be short and easy.

Microsoft Project Standard 2002 is a project management program. It's designed to make it easier for groups of people to work together, exchange information, manage resources, and coordinate schedules.

According to Microsoft, "Project management is often perceived as a complex and difficult business function, and thus the common misconception is that a project management software tool must be complex and difficult to use. Project management is merely a formalization of what many people automatically do everyday. Microsoft Project 2002 has been designed to be easily understood and meet the needs of those new to managing a project. For example, the functions of constructing task lists, tracking the progress of a project, assigning people to carry out the tasks, and also manipulating the task list are all functions that are easily carried out within Microsoft Project 2002, but that would be cumbersome to achieve with Excel."

Using Microsoft Project's "Dynamic Scheduling" feature, Microsoft reports, "you can instantly see the impact of a schedule or resource change on your overall project schedule. With the software's built-in Project Guide, you'll be able to quickly set up a new project, manage tasks and resources, track schedules, and report project information."

Microsoft Project can be used to record and manage information generated during brainstorming sessions, track notes and data relating to the evaluation process for ideas, and then as a valuable tool for managing the implementation of new ideas and making them a reality. Especially when it comes to the implementation process, this software will help you stay on track, on time, and on budget. All of your data can be displayed in a variety of formats, using charts, graphs, and a wide range of customizable reports.

For $8, a 60-day, fully operational version of the Microsoft Project Standard 2002 software can be ordered directly from the Microsoft Website (*www.microsoft.com/office/project/evaluation/trial.asp*).

(Portions of the preceding description were quoted and paraphrased from www.microsoft.com*.)*

FileMaker Pro 6.0

Company: FileMaker, Inc.

Phone: 1-800-325-2747

Website: *www.filemaker.com*

Price: $299

FileMaker Pro 6.0 is a fully customizable workgroup database software application used for creating and sharing a wide range of information, including text and multimedia files (video clips, audio clips, and digital images in a wide range of formats). During and after a brainstorming session, or to manage projects of any size, the software features an easy-to-use interface, making FileMaker Pro 6.0 useful for anyone who needs to track and manage ideas, people, projects, images, and information.

What makes this program unique, according to FileMaker, Inc., is that "FileMaker 6.0 offers the power of a database management program without the need to program. Thanks to the built-in templates that have been designed for a wide range of applications, getting started with this software is fast and easy. The templates can be used to catalog photos, product information, ideas, inventory, to-do lists, budgets, and any other type of records or data."

Once the main database is created, it becomes simple for any number of people to create, organize, and share content over a network or intranet, or to collaborate on multiple projects for greater workgroup productivity.

Data that's incorporated within FileMaker Pro 6.0 can be exchanged with a virtually limitless number of other applications, such as Microsoft Word and Excel, multimedia, and digital image sources. FileMaker Pro 6.0 files can also be transferred to personal digital assistants (PDAs) using the optional FileMaker Mobile 2 software, so data can be accessible from the palm of your hand, virtually anywhere.

As a brainstorming tool, this software is excellent for managing ideas and projects as they are created, and for helping to take an organized approach to implementing those ideas. While this software won't help you generate ideas (and other content), it *will* help you gather, store, organize, manage, and share them. It's best used in a medium to large business environment or by groups working together.

(Portions of the preceding description were quoted and paraphrased from www.filemaker.com.*)*

MindModel

Company: MindModel Corporation

Phone: 1-866-646-3663

Website: *www.mindmodel.com*

Price: $99.95

When it comes to storing and managing facts, figures, data, or ideas (such as those created during a brainstorming session), MindModel is very easy-to-use relational database software package that allows you to store and recall information about any topic.

Within minutes, anyone can create a customized database for storing and managing information about people, companies, products, ideas, or anything else, all without having to do any programming. Sure, there are many database programs on the market. However, this one is particularly simple to use, flexible, and excellent for storing information—lists or ideas, for example— then being able to search those lists based on any criteria. Unlike FileMaker Pro, MindModel is best used by individuals dealing primarily with text-based data (as opposed to images and multimedia content).

(Portions of the preceding description were paraphrased from press materials provided courtesy of the associated company.)

Outlining Made Easy

For many people, creating a written outline is a method of taking notes, generating ideas, and laying the groundwork for a paper, meeting itinerary, letter, report, or presentation, for example. If you use outlines to document your ideas and brainstorming sessions, you'll find an assortment of software packages designed to make creating these glorified lists easier.

Popular word processing programs, such as Microsoft Word, have powerful outlining tools already built in. There are, however, stand-alone outlining software packages available that allow users to create detailed outlines that can be saved, printed, and edited.

Some outlining software packages currently available for PC-based computers include:

- Green Parrot Software's Action Outline 2.0 ($35, *www.greenparrots.com/ao.html*).

- EzO Software's EzOutliner ($49.97, *www.ezoutliner.com*).

- CaseSoft's NoteMap ($99, *www.casesoft.com/notemap*).

- Screenplay Systems, Inc.'s StoryView 2.0 ($99, *www.screenplay.com/products/storyview/index.html*)

- Academix's TakeNote! ($34.95, *www.academixsoft.com/takenote.html*)

A New Way to Brainstorm In Groups

Brainstorming is often a group activity. However, getting a number of people together in the same room to focus on a single issue is often difficult, if not impossible—especially if the people participating in the brainstorming session are located in different offices or even different cities.

Utilizing the latest technologies available though computers, networks, and high-speed Internet connections, Latitude Communications MeetingPlace (1-800-999-7440, *www.meetingplace.net*) is a specialized service that allows people to participate in real-time virtual meetings from anywhere, as long as they're near a telephone and/or a computer that's connected to the Internet. Using MeetingPlace's video and web conferencing capabilities, groups of people can speak and at the same time, and exchange data and text. Documents and graphics can all be created and shared by two or more people working together, even if those people are in totally different places. There's no need to send faxes or e-mails back and forth, because everything happens in real-time, as if you're sitting next to the other people in the meeting.

MeetingPlace breaks down common meeting obstacles and allows people to work together in an organized manner. Thus, brainstorming sessions can take place and ideas can be exchanged with ease. MeetingPlace automatically records all meetings, so the audio, text, and graphic files can all be referred to later. According to the company, "the software also allows for real-time polling of participants, private messaging between two people involved in a group meeting, and software sharing (so an actual [Microsoft] Word document or Excel spreadsheet, for example, can be worked on by several people at once who are in different locations.)"

This application is idea for small, medium, and large companies and is particularly useful for brainstorming sessions where members of the group can't meet in person. The cost (for small business operators) for this service starts at $99 per month, giving up to 25 users unlimited use of MeetingPlace to share and exchange ideas (corporate pricing is also available). This service is more affordable and more interactive than video conferencing and more powerful that traditional Web-based chats or conferences where only text and data can be exchanged in real-time.

(Portions of the preceding description were quoted and paraphrased from www.meetingplace.net.*)*

A less powerful alternative to MeetingPlace is Microsoft NetMeeting (*www.microsoft.com/windows/netmeeting*). This is a free program that allows you to connect a Web cam to your computer and communicate with someone else using real-time video, audio, graphics (whiteboard), file transfers, and text. This program requires that each computer be connected to the Web. It has some definite limitations, especially if you have a slow Internet connection. If two people in separate locations want to brainstorm together, the NetMeeting software could prove helpful when exchanging ideas and collaborating on projects.

Personal Digital Assistants (PDAs)

Imagine the power of a computer in a device that fits in the palm of your hand. Well, even though you're now more of a creative thinker, there's no need to stretch your imagination too far, because these devices are readily available. They're called Personal Digital Assistants or PDAs.

Companies like HandSpring (*www.Handspring.com*) and Palm (*www.Palm.com*) offer PDAs with various built-in applications, such as an electronic address book, scheduler, calculator, to-do list, and memo pad. You can also download thousands of other specialized applications into your PDA, transforming it into a powerful (yet portable) word processor, currency converter, or even a digital diary.

The Palm 515 PDA.

The new wireless PDAs, such as the Palm Tungsten W, for example, even allow you to surf the Internet and send and receive e-mail using a wireless network. The HandSpring Treo 300 offers all of these features, plus a built-in cell phone (compatible with cellular networks such as Sprint PCS, Cingular, T-Mobile, and VoiceStream).

The cost of a PDA ranges from under $200 to over $500, depending on the functionality. Any of these units, however, can be used as a brainstorming tool. With your PDA in-hand, you can jot down ideas (to later transfer to your computer) and store vast amounts of information that is later available at your fingertips. Some units also have a color screen and built-in digital camera, so you can take snapshots, add text captions, and either store this information or transfer it to a PC or via the Internet.

The Handspring Treo 300 PDA with built-in cell phone.

As an organizational and productivity tool, these devices are indispensable once you start using one. For the brainstormer, they offer an alternative to carrying around a pad and pen, plus the ability to store, manage, and transfer notes and information with ease.

In a group brainstorming situation, for example, if each person is equipped with a Palm PDA, data can easily be "beamed" back and forth between units using infrared technology.

There are even optional brainstorming, idea-organization, and outlining applications that can be added to the PDA, such as:

🐾 Palm Learning, Inc.'s IdeaPad ($14.95, *http://software.palm.com/*). Idea Pad lets you easily draw a diagram, such as a mind map, concept map, or flow chart, then convert it to a text outline or vice versa. Diagrams can be exported to any desktop graphics program, while text-based outlines can be exported to any word processor via the PDA's built-in "Memo Pad." Use Idea Pad to brainstorm new ideas, illustrate concepts, plan presentations, and create organizational charts. *(Portions of this description are paraphrased from* http://software.palm.com/.)

🐾 HandsHigh Software's Thought Manager ($19.95, *www.Handshigh.com*) is another excellent PDA software package for brainstormers and creative thinkers. This software will easily organize your ideas, project plans, agendas, meeting notes, task lists, speeches, shopping lists, class outlines, and lots more. Free your mind from thinking about all the details of the day and put them into Thought Manager. A PC version of this software is also available, so your ideas can be synchronized between your PC and PDA with ease. *(Portions of this description are paraphrased from* www.Handshigh.com.)

🐾 Aportis Technologies Corp.'s BrainForest ($30, *www.aportis.com*) is an action item organizer, outliner, idea tracker, project planner, and checklist manager, that uses a tree analogy to organize information into hierarchical and intuitive trees, branches, and leaves—a structure similar to the "Outline" function in Microsoft Word. This program allows for complete customization of data views on any Palm Computing platform device. Branches and leaves may be given a priority, start date, due date, and check box (or completion percentage), with the ability to have any item recur automatically. Information stored within BrainForest can be sorted in several flexible ways. "Show" and "Hide" options permit the display of all items or the selective display of only items that are due or urgent. Notes can also be maintained for every item. *(Portions of this description are paraphrased from* www.aportis.com.)

Recently, PDAs have dropped in price, yet their capabilities have increased dramatically. No matter what your needs, these are powerful, yet relatively easy-to-use tools that are an excellent extension for a desktop computer or even a laptop. After all, these units fit in a pocket and weight just a few ounces.

Seiko's InkLink Handwriting System

Imagine taking notes on a regular 8 1/2 x 11 notepad, and then having those notes be easily transferable onto your computer or PDA screen to be edited or stored. Your own handwritten notes, sketches, and ideas can all be transferred to a computer when you use Seiko Instrument's InkLink Handwriting System (1-800-688-0817, *www.seikosmart.com*). For less than $100, the InkLink system includes a special clip that attaches to the top of any notepad. You also receive a special pen/stylus, which you'll use for note taking.

When you're ready to transfer what you've created on paper to your computer, you simply connect the pad's clip to the PC or PDA using an infrared transfer or a USB connector. Within moments, your notes can be edited or viewed on your computer screen. The InkLink Handwriting System comes with InkNote Manager software to give you added functionality once your notes are created.

You can always take your handwritten notes and scan them into your computer, but the InkNote Handwriting System is designed to make the process easier and faster, while also giving you added control over the notes and images once they've been transferred to the computer or PDA.

Users have the freedom to organize their notes according to their personal preferences, including date, time, category names, keywords, or other user preferences. Additionally, you can edit, cut, copy, paste, group/ungroup, undo/redo, draw straight lines, and even write or highlight in seven colors. InkNote Manager automatically saves users' notes as ".ink" vector files, but also allows the files to be exported into BMP, PNG, and JPG formats for use with many popular Windows-based applications.

SMART Board

The SMART Board (1-888-42-SMART, *www.smarttech.com*) is a more high-tech version of the dry erase board. The SMART Board interactive whiteboard turns your computer and projector into a powerful tool for teaching, collaborating, and presenting. Information written on the board's surface can be automatically and instantly saved to a computer file. This functionality ensures that your ideas will not be lost and can be accessed and reviewed at any time. Saving your ideas to a computer file also eliminates the need for individual note-taking during the session and leaves brainstorming participants focused on idea-generation.

The pace of the brainstorming session can be so quick that the facilitator has difficulty keeping the ideas legible and organized on the page. Because any notes written on the SMART Board are recorded as separate objects, the information can be easily rearranged or edited after the session. This makes it easy for a facilitator to clean up the notes before e-mailing or printing them for distribution to the meeting participants. SMART Boards are available in several sizes and are most useful when working in a group situation.

Rhymex Clocks

One method of brainstorming is to use random words as triggers in your mind to create associations and develop new ideas. To select a random word, you can open a dictionary to a random page. You can also use a Magnetic Poetry set (*www.MagneticPoetry.com*). Another alternative, however, is to use a Rhymex Clock from Rhymex World Clocks (*www.rhymex.com*).

The Random Word Clock is a custom made piece of functional art. The clock concept was invented and refined by Miles Grenadier throughout the 1990s and was recently brought to life with electronics. Each clock is hand-built and guaranteed to be unique. The clocks store words that are shown as random pairs—you never know what will be shown next. Each clock is battery-powered, making it portable and easy to display anywhere.

The Writer's Block ($320) is ideal for the aspiring or professional writer who may occasionally need inspiration. This clock has a switch that makes the word on the display change with a slight tap. The solid wood case has a natural craft-style appearance. This clock is offered with a beautiful teal-blue vacuum fluorescent display. The display is self-illuminating and can easily be seen day and night from five to 10 feet away. The clock is a perfect cube, measuring 4 x 4 x 4 inches. It's designed to run continuously.

The Traveler ($79) is a smaller, more rugged version of The Writer's Block. It fits easily in a pocket, making it perfect for hiking, camping, or just handing around a dinner table to help get a conversation started. This clock comes with a high-contrast LCD display. This version has a 3-way toggle switch so that you can select from lit and non-lit mode. Just click the switch and a new word pair will be displayed. The clock is mounted in a black plastic enclosure and will display thousands of word pairs on one battery.

Developing Your Brainstorming Toolbox

Not every tool described in this chapter is useful for every purpose. The trick to effectively utilizing one or more of these brainstorming tools is to determine your needs for each situation and then to take advantage of the tools that you believe can make you more productive as you brainstorm or put your ideas into motion. Over time, you'll develop your own brainstorming toolbox, comprised of items that can help you brainstorm in different types of situations. Whether you're brainstorming alone or with a group of people, these tools can help you address problems and confront challenges in more organized ways as you find creative solutions and generate awesome new ideas.

Sometimes, however, when a group of people gets together to brainstorm, things don't work out as planned. Distractions can take place and people can lack creativity or lose their focus. In these situations, you might consider utilizing the services of a *brainstorming facilitator*. Brainstorming facilitators are professional creative thinkers and organizers who can offer guidance and training. You'll learn more about what these people do and whether or not you might benefit from hiring one in the next chapter.

CHAPTER 9

Brainstorming Facilitators: Hiring a Professional

Believe it or not, there are people whose job is to help others, such as yourself, become better brainstormers and more creative thinkers. These people offer a wide range of services to individuals and to companies of all sizes—typically offering instruction and guidance to enhance creativity in order to solve problems.

A brainstorming facilitator is very different from a meeting facilitator. A meeting or function facilitator is often hired to oversee a business meeting or gathering, make sure things stay on track, provide the tools that are needed for the meeting (computers, projectors, white boards, etc.), make sure the catering arrives on time, and insure that everyone's needs are met.

A brainstorming facilitator is someone who steps into a group situation and actually guides that group to use creativity and brainstorming techniques in order to achieve a specific goal or objective. For example, a company may require help developing ideas for new products.

When companies run into situations where creativity or a different way of thinking is required, but the know-how or skill set is not possessed by someone within the company, a brainstorming facilitator can be brought in, not to create the idea that is needed, but to help the people within a company to develop and implement their own ideas.

Finding a Brainstorming Facilitator

The very best way to find a brainstorming facilitator is to obtain a referral from an individual or company that has already used one. The Internet is also an excellent tool for locating someone to work with. Using any Web search engine (such as Yahoo.com or Google.com), enter one of these search phrases:

- Brainstorming facilitator.
- Creative problem-solving.
- Creativity consultant.
- Creativity guru.
- Innovation consultant.
- Innovation process leader.

Before actually hiring someone, make sure he or she has excellent credentials and proven experience doing the types of brainstorming you need or want to do. Understand what your objectives are, then find someone who can help you achieve those objectives.

Keep in mind, someone with extensive experience working with well-known Fortune 500 companies may have no experience working for a 10-person start-up, a dot-com company, a small family-owned business, a writer, or an artist.

It's always a good strategy to meet with a brainstorming facilitator for an introductory session to determine if the person who will offer consulting is a good match for your company (or you as an individual). Creativity and brainstorming facilitation is an industry in itself. There are many consultants offering many different services all relating to creativity, innovation, and brainstorming. A good facilitator will make happen what you want and need to happen.

A Closer Look at Two Brainstorming Facilitation Firms

What you're about to read are interviews with executives from Synectics, Inc. and Basadur Applied Creativity, two independent brainstorming facilitation firms which are pioneers in their field. These firms have reputations for helping some of the best known companies in the world. In these interviews, two creativity and brainstorming experts share their advice for hiring a brainstorming facilitator and also provide tips for successful idea generation.

Jeff Mauzy

Synectics, Inc./Inventive Logic, Inc.

Phone: 1-617-868-6530

Website: *www.synecticsworld.com*

SYNECTICS®

Synectics Logo

Inventive Logic Logo

Background

Jeff Mauzy, a principal at Synectics, Inc. (and Chairman of Inventive Logic, Inc.), explained that his company's work is all about helping its clients create and discover new ideas, new thinking, new behaviors, and new ways of working. Synectics has discovered, through experience, that the insights on how to achieve this are lying dormant within the minds of its clients. Thus, it's the job of Synectics to help draw the new ideas out and help those ideas take on a practical shape.

Synectics tends to work exclusively with large corporations around the world, such as 3M, American Express, Audi, Citigroup, Coca-Cola, Reebok, Kellogg's, Harvard Medical School, IBM, Mars, NATO, Nabisco, Nestlé, and Shell Oil.

Jeffrey Mauzy

Even if you can't afford to hire Jeff and his team, you can take full advantage of their research and knowledge, not just by reading this interview, but also by obtaining and using a copy of the ThoughtPath software (published by Inventive Logic), which is described in greater detail in Chapter 8. This software was developed using many of the same principles, exercises, and lessons taught to top-level executives by Jeff and the specialists working for Synectics.

(Some information within the previous section is from press material provided courtesy of the associated individual or company.)

Interview With Jeff Mauzy

Q: Do you develop ideas for the client, or help them create their own ideas?

JM: Our basic assumption is that you know more about your business than we do. We believe that you have the content knowledge already. What we offer is know-how about the process of innovation. In short, we act as catalysts to help you think about new ways of helping yourself. We believe that everyone has the ability to be creative and to innovate. The problem is, these intuitive skills are often suppressed by education, cultural conditioning, and misplaced competitiveness.

Q: What does it take to help people or companies generate awesome ideas?

JM: We have developed a wide range of customizable programs and exercises we use. One of our goals is to totally eliminate the negative things that kill creativity. For example, people need to be personally motivated to think most creatively. Just paying them doesn't work quite as well—that's not personal enough. They need to be thinking about issues and problems, for example, that they understand, relate to, and believe in. We also strive to drastically decrease the level of fear associated with creative thinking, brainstorming, analyzing ideas, and implementing them.

Q: What are the biggest mistakes you see companies make when adopting creative thinking strategies?

JM: One major mistake is that people expect instant results. We work in a society that demands fast answers. We're forced to work under tight deadlines. If you're in a rush, you'll be forced to make compromises, and those compromises usually come at the expense of the freshest thinking. It's important for people to take the time to be creative and allow the process to work.

Q: What happens when people who are trying to be creative experience the equivalent to writer's block?

JM: This is often caused by a fear. People are afraid of failure, or of not being relevant enough, or of being laughed at for their ideas. There are strategies, such as using excursionary techniques [mental triggers], or metaphor, or role play, that help people enhance their creativity, but the first step is to eliminate those real or perceived fears that are blocking your success. When someone or a group of people is brainstorming, the worst mistake that can be made is evaluating, critiquing, and analyzing the ideas too quickly, while ideas are still being created. Instantly evaluating a new idea is what most people automatically do, and that's the wrong approach to take.

Q: What's the best way to analyze ideas once they're generated?

JM: My flip answer is, "Don't try!" Often people evaluate ideas based on the wrong criteria. For example, people can analyze an idea based upon newness, intrigue, and workability. These criteria are often in opposition to each other. The really new and interesting ideas are the ones you've never tried, and you haven't tried them because they seem unworkable for one reason or another. When most people talk about objectively looking at an idea, they're usually talking about gauging them on the feasibility scale, based on what's already the accepted norm. This tends to cause ideas that are basically extensions of already existing ideas to be created, as opposed to totally new, breakthrough, and fresh ideas. It *is* possible to overanalyze an idea. People who analyze too deeply or too quickly, and too early, are going to shoot themselves in the foot.

Q: What are some of the reasons why a company would hire Synectics?

JM: We help companies achieve a wide range of objectives. For example, we worked with a major financial institution a few years back to help them develop new ways to solve the Y2K problem. They already had a strategy in place, but wanted us to help them determine if there were breakthrough ideas that hadn't yet been considered. We also helped a major oil company brainstorm before it began building a new refinery. The designers wanted to know if there were any new ideas that could be incorporated into the design of the refinery, before it was actually built. Companies have also hired us to help them develop new markets for existing products, develop ideas for new products, or come up with a plan to drastically reduce costs without having to lay off people. We often help companies solve problems as well as pinpoint and go after new opportunities.

Q: If someone wants to hire a company like yours, what should they consider beforehand?

JM: One thing that needs to be considered is the chemistry between the people at the company and our people. Our job can put our clients through hell. They come to us with a problem, and we often turn their world upside down looking for a breakthrough idea. We ask our clients to go out on a limb sometimes, when they're desperate for a solution. This can cause a tremendous amount of stress. The client has to trust us and our skills.

They have to trust that we are working for their company. Although the client remains in charge ultimately, there are times they need to let go and trust the person they have hired for this, and this is when chemistry becomes critical. You, as the client, need to know you can trust the people you're hiring and that they understand what your problem is that you're trying to solve. In addition to working with clients, at Synectics, we continue to research both creativity and innovation, which is the application of creativity, which then gets applied to our work for our clients.

When you first approach a brainstorming facilitator, for example, make them convince you not only that they can help you, but explain how they plan to do this. You need to be convinced the approach they plan to take will work. I don't believe price should be a factor when deciding whom to hire. If the process works, you'll receive a positive return on your investment. The deciding factor about who you hire should be based upon the results you anticipate achieving. The cheapest option won't always allow you to achieve those objectives.

Finally, when hiring someone to help your business be more creative, for whatever reason, don't shortchange the process. Don't expect instant results in a few hours after the consultant comes to your office. Many people want results that are fast, cheap, and good. Well, when you're involved with innovation, brainstorming, and creative thinking, these three demands typically can't go together.

Dr. Min Basadur

Basadur Applied Creativity

Phone: 1-888-88-SOLVE

Web Site: *www.basadur.com*

Background

Founded by Dr. Min Basadur and comprised of brainstorming facilitators and creativity experts from around the globe, Basadur Applied Creativity is a network of highly trained professionals who have helped hundreds of companies restructure how they operate, harness the power of creative thinking, and generate proven results.

Dr. Min Basadur is Professor of Innovation at the Michael G. DeGroote School of Business at McMaster University, in Hamilton, Ontario. He is also the Founder of Basadur Applied Creativity, which has corporate offices in Cincinnati and Toronto.

Dr. Basadur is a recognized world leader in the field of applied creativity. He has years of experience in building creative thinking, innovation, and problem-solving. Thus far in his career, he has helped hundreds of industry leaders, including Procter & Gamble, Frito-Lay, PepsiCo, and Ford, to involve employees at every level in using their creativity to generate hundreds of millions of dollars in new revenues and cost savings.

Dr. Min Basadur

Educated in organizational psychology and engineering physics, Dr. Basadur began refining his insights about creative thinking and problem solving while working with teams developing new products at Procter & Gamble. He later created the award-winning Simplex System with its unique set of interconnected tools.

Today Dr. Basadur and his associates work with clients engaged in a range of industries, including software, microelectronics, telecommunications, finance, health, food and beverage, publishing, energy, retail, manufacturing, e-commerce, and many others.

In this interview, Dr. Basadur shares his advice on who should hire a professional brainstorming facilitator. He also explains what a brainstorming facilitator does and offers detailed tips and strategies for implementing some of the proven creative-thinking strategies he and his colleagues have spent decades developing. These techniques are currently in use by hundreds of companies throughout North America and the world.

(Some information within the previous section is from press material provided courtesy of the associated individual or company.)

Interview With Dr. Min Basadur

Q: How did you get started working in the brainstorming and creativity consulting business?

MB: My background is in engineering physics, which is what I studied in college. Upon graduation, I began working for Proctor & Gamble's research and development department in Canada. I believed out of all the companies I interviewed with, the position I was offered seemed to be the most interesting. It allowed me to keep my career options open. Working in R&D provided a relatively unstructured environment, which I ultimately prospered in. I really began to enjoy my work developing new products. During those years, I discovered that I was a *horizontal thinker* as opposed to a *vertical thinker*, which set me apart from the other people I was working with.

After working in Canada for about six years, I was invited to work at Proctor & Gamble's corporate offices in Cincinnati, Ohio. At the time, the company was at a point where it needed an influx of creativity. Revenues and growth were flat. I was selected to learn how creativity could be infused into the company. I attended many seminars and, within the company, started my own consulting practice. My job was to train the various divisions and departments within Proctor & Gamble to think more creativity.

For the next nine years, I worked as a consultant within almost every division of Proctor & Gamble. I also obtained three U.S. Patents for my own work. In time, I discovered that what I wanted to do with my life is help others, including organizations, become more innovative. In pursuit of this goal, I attended the University of Cincinnati and participated in the school's Management Ph.D. program. My dissertation about creativity and creative problem solving won a national award from The American Psychological Association. At this time [the 1980s], I was an internal consultant with Proctor & Gamble, but I began receiving calls from Ford Motors, General Foods, Goodyear Tires, and other companies looking to hire me. This is when Basadur Applied Creativity was formed.

Q: Who have been some of your more notable clients?

MB: In addition to Proctor & Gamble, I've worked with Frito-Lay, PepsiCo, Ford Motors, Canon, IBM, General Mills, TRW, USA Today, and countless other companies, of all sizes and throughout the world. What all of these companies share is that their senior management believes innovation is something that can work. Brainstorming isn't about fun and games. It's about identifying and achieving an actual business purpose. Innovation, like efficiency, can become a normal business function within the organization.

Q: **Earlier, you mentioned you consider yourself to be a** *horizontal thinker*. **What does this mean and how does it differ from being a** *vertical thinker*?

MB: A *horizontal thinker* is like a project manager. It's someone who can conceive of an idea and move that idea through every division within an organization to make it a reality. Most organizations are divided into silos. For example, there's a manufacturing department, R&D department, marketing department, and sales department, all of which have very defined roles within the organization. Someone in R&D doesn't care what the marketing department does. The people working in each division are typically *vertical thinkers*. They are only concerned about achieving distinct goals within their division. An R&D department may develop an idea for a product, but for that product to become a reality, it then goes to the Engineering Department, for example. It's like a relay race. Each division does its work and passes the project on to the next division. A horizontal thinker looks at the whole process and sees his job as moving the idea through each silo within the organization until the final product reaches the customer at the end. This person doesn't care about the goals of each individual department or silo, he or she cares about the big picture. Most companies have few or no horizontal thinkers or true project managers. Companies wind up having to bring in these people from the outside, mainly because, in-house, there is a lot of resistance to these people.

Q: **For a typical company that needs or wants to enhance its creativity, do you recommend hiring a brainstorming facilitator?**

MB: That's what we do. It's our primary business, so yes, I do. We teach companies how to brainstorm and build creative self-sufficiency. We do three types of work. First, we work as brainstorming facilitators to help a company achieve one specific goal or objective. We don't do the work for them. Instead, we provide the guidance an organization needs to develop its own ideas. This short-term process we call "Creativity In Action."

The second type of work we do is help people within an organization develop their brainstorming and creativity skills. We do this not to solve a particular problem, but to educate a company on how to work more innovatively. This is where we actually teach brainstorming skills and techniques.

Finally, we also help companies make creativity a way of life. This involves what we call an "Innovation Audit," where we go to the company, sit down with them, and determine what it means to be innovative.

We determine what challenges it's facing without innovation, and have the company define innovation in its own terms. This is all done with the client's senior management. An innovation might be to increase the number of new products that come to market each year. This is a defined need that we then help the client develop a program to achieve, based upon its internal resources. This process involves much more than just teaching brainstorming techniques.

Q: When it comes to teaching brainstorming skills, where do you begin?

MB: Brainstorming is all about what we call "active divergence," or "problem-finding," and being able to discover problems people or organizations have that they don't even know they have. The next step is the "problem-solving" phase, which means coming up with the processes, technologies, and products that will help solve those identified problems. Finally, it involves implementation of the new ideas and solutions.

Our job isn't to do the brainstorming for people or clients, it's to teach them how to fish for themselves, so to speak. Very often, an organization is willing to talk a good game about needing to be more innovative and creative, but it's not really willing to do anything to accomplish this. Our goal is to teach the skills necessary so companies become self-sufficient when implementing creativity. Our tag line is "Revolutionizing how people think."

Q; How do you describe the perfect client for Basadur Applied Creativity?

MB: It's a company that is truly interested in having a more innovative organization in the long-term. It's a company that is willing to take the time to diagnose what its innovation problems are, to develop a good strategy for innovation, and to work hard to engage its senior management to develop the necessary skills for creative thinking. Most companies already have plenty of top-notch analytical thinkers. What they need are people who are willing to learn how to master skills for creative and innovative thinking. Becoming an innovative company requires a lot more than putting a sign or banner up on the wall instructing employees to "think creatively," which is all a lot of companies do.

In terms of company size, we work with organizations of all sizes and from all industries. We adapt what we do to fit the needs of each client from what we offer to what we charge for our services.

Q: What skills do you specifically teach your clients?

MB: We teach what we call "active divergence." This is the ability to deliberately create options in any kind of a situation. Those options include seeing different points of view and creating or identifying new problems that need to be solved. We also teach how to create different problem definitions or ways to define a problem or opportunity. We do not differentiate between problems, opportunities, and trends. These are all good things that fall under "problem finding."

The world's greatest inventors have always been good, not so much at finding solutions, but at discovering good problems to solve. We also teach methods for overcoming resistance to new ideas. All of this active divergence is done non-analytically and non-judgmentally. The willingness to accept other points of view is critical for this type of thinking.

The second major skill we teach is "active convergence." This is the reverse of active divergence. It's the ability to open-mindedly evaluate options that have been developed and to wisely separate the more promising options from the ones that are less promising. This involves developing unbiased criteria for making those kinds of choices, and then doing what it takes to move ahead in the process.

The third skill we teach is how to separate active divergence and active convergence. This is the ability to deliberately defer judgment or logic. This avoids one person shooting down another person's idea and laying out all of the reasons why an idea won't work. It's important for a group to systematically diverge and then later converge again. The fundamental process is one that involves continuously identifying new problems, generating new opportunities, conceptualizing fuzzy ideas, and then creating well-defined definitions of the opportunity to be solved. Albert Einstein once said that if he had one hour to save the world, he would spend 55 minutes defining and conceptualizing the problem and only five minutes solving it.

Later, we train people to evaluate potential good solutions that come from the conceptualization phase, then solve the problem using a very well-defined plan that is most likely to work.

Finally, we teach implementation. This means taking the new solution and implementing it into the company and staying with it until all resistance is overcome. All of these stages must be completed as part of the innovation process. Once a solution to a problem is implemented, it always leads to new problems to confront, so there is a never-ending cycle of new opportunities for organizations that choose to pinpoint and capitalize on them.

The skills and the basic process I just described will work within any organization. In everything we do, we push for simplicity. We assume that everyone is creative, however, we know that some people are more creative as generators, optimizers, or conceptualizers, while others work better as implementers of new ideas. Unless you have people filling all of these needs within an organization, new ideas will not be created and successfully put into use.

Q: **What you just described would work nicely for people brainstorming in a group situation. Do the same steps apply to individuals working on their own to create or innovate?**

MB: Yes. All of the same principles apply. Thomas Edison, for example, had to do everything I just described by himself. The greatest artists, for example, spend a lot of time generating the problem, conceptualizing it, and then painting it. We think of the process working at three levels—the individual, the team, and the organization as a whole. When you're working as an individual, you're not encumbered by other people. There's nobody to get in the way. When you're dealing with a team, there are people around you who share different points of view, but you have to coordinate how these people work together without getting in the way of each other.

Q: **When someone is trying to be creative, how important is creating a conducive environment for brainstorming?**

MB: It certainly helps. We have an innovations center that allows people to customize their environment. For example, we can turn the lights down, play music, give people lots of room to roam freely, and we provide white boards for people to express themselves. The better you create an environment that allows people to get away from their everyday work, the better it is. We try to get people out of their ordinary environment, away from interruptions, such as the telephone. Many companies find it useful to develop their own innovation centers in-house.

Q: **How does fear limit someone's ability to brainstorm and be creative?**

MB: People need to learn how good it feels to generate ideas and opinions without someone else putting them down. It often takes training to overcome the fear associated with voicing your own opinions. If someone is afraid to be innovative or voice their opinions, the ability to generate ideas diminishes dramatically. After all of the ideas have been created, without thinking about logic or judgment, that's when you can offer critique.

In a group environment, I suggest posting some defined rules at the very start. Make it clear that there will be no passing judgment on ideas. The goal, initially, should be for developing a quantity of ideas, and for people to build on each other's ideas. It should be a facilitator's job to make sure these rules are strictly enforced.

Q: **What do you recommend when someone experiences "brainstormer's block" and has trouble generating new ideas?**

MB: A lot of times, when this happens, it's just a matter of making people feel more secure in the environment in which they're working. To overcome "brainstormer's block" we have a strategy called "W.I.O.," which stands for "Wild Ideas Only." We have people start off by creating only the wackiest, most outrageous ideas they can think of. The first 10 ideas, for example, must be wacky ones. This is a great way to get people to open their minds. Generally, people are too judgmental of themselves or each other, and that's what causes brainstormer's block. It's easier to make a good idea out of a wild one than it is to take a very practical idea and make it more innovative or creative.

Once people have their 10 wacky ideas, they should be challenged to come up with several things that are good about each of those ideas. The bad things about the idea are not allowed to be discussed. We always find that people can come up with good things about the wackiest of ideas, then take those ideas and develop new ideas. The wacky ideas act as building blocks to get the creative thinking going. If several groups are working together in one room, each group can take its single wackiest idea and trade. The next group must then build upon the other group's wackiest idea.

Another technique is to do an activity we call "unclumping." Some ideas are very broad or general. We encourage people to generate more specific ideas that break down the general idea. For example, if we're working with a car manufacturer and the idea is to make a car more comfortable, we turn around and ask for ideas about all of the ways this can be achieved.

Q: **How important is goal-setting in a brainstorming session?**

MB: This can be extremely helpful. People can achieve amazing things if they're working toward a defined goal or milestone. To get people brainstorming, a goal might be to generate 150 new ideas, or 10 additional ideas above and beyond what's already been done. While defining a goal is helpful, establishing a tight deadline is not always conducive to brainstorming because some people freeze up under pressure.

Q: Is it possible to make mistakes when brainstorming?

MB: The only mistake you can make is not following the rules and being too critical of ideas too quickly. Brainstorming is a process. Not criticizing other people's ideas is important, but you must also not inwardly criticize or prejudge your own ideas so that you're afraid to share them. When this happens, it is an error of omission, and that's common.

Q: During a brainstorming session, what tools do you recommend people use?

MB: Those large flip-chart pads that go on easels are excellent brainstorming tools. You must, however, post everything that's put on paper. Every time a sheet of paper gets filled up, it should be posted up on the wall for everyone to see. The goal is to look at ideas that have been generated and keep building upon them. It's the facilitator's job to make sure that everything gets written down.

In addition to physical tools, I encourage people to use all five of their senses as tools. Think of things you've seen, touched, heard, smelled, and tasted, in order to consider problems and solutions from a different perspective. There are things you can do that will trigger more creativity and innovation. We have developed many exercises to help trigger people's creativity and thinking process.

Q: Is there any other advice you'd like to share about brainstorming or hiring a brainstorming facilitator?

MB: Make sure you understand what you're trying to achieve through brainstorming, and understanding how this activity will fit into your existing company structure. If you want people to think innovatively in teams, your company's reward structure, for example, should compensate people for thinking well in teams. If necessary, bring in a consultant to help you figure out what you're trying to do through innovative thinking. Create a roadmap in advance about where you're going and how creativity can help you.

In the next two chapters you'll have a chance to learn from ordinary people who have achieved extraordinary success as a result of their ability to brainstorm and think creatively.

CHAPTER 10

Brainstorming Success Stories From Arts and Entertainment

Throughout this book, you've read about strategies for enhancing your creativity, you've learned how to brainstorm, and you've discovered the importance of being an innovative thinker in every aspect of your life. Within this chapter and the next, you'll read in-depth interviews with highly successful people, from all walks of life, who have achieved success as a direct result of their ability to brainstorm, tap into their creativity, and transform their innovative ideas into reality.

You're about to read several interviews with people who have artistic backgrounds—a well-known television personality, a cartoonist, an artist, and a recording artist (singer/songwriter/pianist). The next chapter features interviews with people who tap into their creativity and ability to brainstorm to achieve success in a more traditional business environment.

From all of these interviews, you'll see firsthand that brainstorming and creative thinking are activities anyone can do to achieve a wide range of positive results. You'll also discover what inspires these people and how they transform that inspiration into reality in order to achieve success. Most importantly, you'll be able to learn from these people and discover their strategies for success.

In your own life, you may know creative thinkers and be able to look up to them as role models. Whether or not this is the case, the people interviewed in this book offer perfect examples of how brainstorming and creativity can be used to help people transform their dreams into reality. As you read these interviews, allow yourself to learn from the experience of others and to be inspired!

Tom Bergeron

Occupation: Television Personality—Host of *Hollywood Squares* and *America's Funniest Home Videos*

Websites: *www.HollywoodSquares.com* and *www.AFHV.com*

Background

Tom Bergeron is an award-winning television and radio personality with over 30 years experience in broadcasting. He can currently be seen as the host

Television Personality Tom Bergeron

of the syndicated television game show *Hollywood Squares,* as well as the host of ABC-TV's prime-time series *America's Funniest Home Videos.* Occasionally, you can also catch Tom as a guest host of CBS-TV's *The Early Show.* Tom recently showed off his acting ability when he guest starred as an alien on the popular UPN-TV *Star Trek* series, *Enterprise*, during its first season.

While Tom has achieved long-term success as a television host because of his charm, wit, intelligence, and upbeat personality, one of his most useful skills continues to be his ability to brainstorm, plus come up with creative ideas and quickly implement them during live broadcasts. In this interview, Tom shares some of his secrets for creative thinking, a lot of which, he says, comes down to being relaxed and totally prepared when put on the spot.

Interview With Tom Bergeron

Q: **How did you know you had what it took to be a host on live television or radio?**

TB: Early on, I didn't know I had these skills. All I knew was that this is what I really wanted to do. I felt a real pull, first to radio, then to improvisational theater, and ultimately toward television. I was working in radio for about five years before I came to believe I had certain skills in communication and improvisation that allowed me to be successful during live broadcasts. Whether I am hosting a game show or a news show, what I strive to do is enjoy myself in the moment. When I'm living in the moment and experiencing the Zen of the moment, especially during a live broadcast, the ability to think quickly, clearly, and creatively occurs naturally for me.

Q: **Did you ever pursue any type of education to enhance your creative thinking or brainstorming skills?**

TB: I received my very best training as a broadcaster from a mime. I studied mime from Tony Montanaro, who operates the Montanaro-Hurll theatre of Mime and Dance in Maine [*www.mimetheatre.com*]. He helped me find my own direction and taught me how to express myself on stage. He critiqued our performances based on how committed and connected we were to the material and how willing we were to take chances on stage. That really reinforced everything I do in broadcasting. It taught me to be present in the moment and never to simply go through the motions. He also taught us never to overanalyze ourselves or allow our analytical mind to get in the way of our creativity.

Q: **When you're hosting a live broadcast, you have to think quickly, be creative, and always be on your toes. How do you prepare for that?**

TB: When I fill in as a guest host on *The Early Show*, for example, the night before the live broadcast, I go into what I call "sponge mode." I use the time to prepare myself by taking in as much information as possible about the next day's guests and segments. Once I've processed this information the night before, I stop actively thinking about it. When it's time to do the show, I just try to have a normal conversation with the guests, for example, trusting the information I gathered and entered into my mind the night before will be there when and if it's needed. I try to avoid thinking too much about prepared interview questions, for example.

For every show I do, I always consider the format of the program and what my limitations are, then direct my performance so it fits within the predefined framework. I always try to play with the boundaries of the show's parameters to keep things interesting and fresh from a creative standpoint.

One morning on *The Early Show*, I knew I'd be interviewing Tom Ridge about the Department of Homeland Security. The night before, I watched a few of his previous interviews. I noticed that he had certain stock answers to questions that he kept using. I needed to brainstorm ways to make my interview different. What I did was take his stock answers and incorporate them into my questions. This forced him to re-think his answers a bit. It threw him off just enough, so I was able to get fresh answers and cover different material with him. In this case, I used brainstorming to see what was there in advance, and then used it to my advantage.

Q: **When you're thinking creatively or brainstorming to prepare for a broadcast, how does this differ from how your mind is working during a live broadcast?**

TB: During a live broadcast, I try to keep my brain from getting in the way and overanalyzing everything. I stay focused on what's happening around me and look for opportunities and things I can work off of in a fun and positive way. A lot has to do with going on impulses and trusting my instincts.

When we're brainstorming in advance of a show, such as an episode of *America's Funniest Home Videos*, we do some communal brainstorming to create ideas for segments, but I also do a lot of brainstorming on my own. I tend to prefer brainstorming myself. At this point in my career, my concern isn't about how one job will lead to the next one, or whether or not a show I work on achieves high ratings. My objective is to have fun and enjoy what I do. That enjoyment allows me to be more creative and excited about what I'm doing.

Q: **When you're doing a live broadcast and you're forced to think creatively on your feet, is there a specific process you go through in your mind?**

TB: At the risk of sounding too esoteric, when I do this well, it's like I'm in some sort of meditation. During a live broadcast, there are many elements at play simultaneously. I try to find ways to tie things together in a fun way. Instead of actively brainstorming during a live broadcast, I try mind sweeping, so my mind is clear. The brainstorming typically happens before the broadcast when I'm preparing. You can't let your ego get in the way of anything. It's all about relaxing, letting things happen, and going with your instincts.

Q: **Once you've experienced a brainstorming session and have generated what you think are good ideas, how do you sell those ideas to other people you work with, such as the producers, for example?**

TB: It comes down to demonstrating a passion for the idea and being willing to act as the guinea pig for the idea's implementation. I'll say something like, "Let me go out there and try it. If it doesn't work, I'm the one who will take the heat." I might also ask for help from the other person, by asking for their assistance in expanding upon or improving my idea. If someone provides their input, they're more apt to buy into the idea as a whole and support it.

In some situations, you might want to take full responsibility for the outcome of your idea, but that depends on the situation. Ultimately, to sell an idea to others, you have to show you're truly passionate about it, believe in it, and feel you can pull it off successfully. I typically won't go out on a limb to push for my own idea, unless I know in my heart the approach that's currently being taken is wrong.

Q: **Do you have any suggestions for people who are forced to brainstorm or be creative under tight deadlines or pressure?**

TB: Yes. When you're doing live television, the starting time for the show is your deadline and it can't be moved. I always prepare in advance, so when it's show time, I can totally relax and trust that I have the confidence, professionalism, and command of the needed information to successfully execute the job at hand. Proper planning and treating deadlines with respect will help eliminate the pressure associated with them. The easiest part of my job is actually doing the live broadcast. The hardest part is preparing in advance for that show and working my way toward the deadline. The period before a broadcast is prep time. I take this time very seriously.

Q: **What is the biggest challenge you face when trying to be creative?**

TB: My biggest challenge is keeping my energy focused and not getting cranky about it. When I go back and look at tapes of past shows I've hosted, I can tell when I had let something distract me. There are subtle differences in my body language that I notice when my mind isn't properly focused.

Like so many people, I also vacillate between a carefree personality and someone who is overly analytical about things. I have to be careful when that analytical part of me sneaks in.

Q: **What happens when you need to be creative but, for whatever reason, the ideas don't flow?**

TB: There have been days when we shoot five episodes of *Hollywood Squares* in a single day and I get tired or find myself to be in a bad mood. It's during these times when I have to force myself to ignore the mood I am in and, at the same time, not try to be funny. If I try too hard and force myself to be funny, for example, it won't work. Those are the days when I make an effort to work off of and be entertained by the other people on the show. More often than not, if I allow myself to relax, instead of trying to fight my way through it, something happens to turn the situation around. For example, someone will make me laugh, and that will get me thinking.

I know that if I try too hard to be funny, I might make a total ass of myself. Thus, when I'm not in the perfect mood, I relax my mind, and I can usually find a back door entrance into the right state of mind that works for me.

Q: **What advice do you have for someone who wants to be more creative in their thinking?**

TB: Get out of your head as much as you can. Find a way to bring some joy to what you're doing. Discover whatever it is about what you're doing that has the ability to bring you pleasure and go with it. Also, try to compete with yourself more than with the rest of the world. Finally, try to live in the moment as much as you possibly can. That's where the real opportunities and rewards are. The more I am worrying about where I am going to be in six months, for example, the less I am paying attention to what's happening around me right now. By not paying attention, you could be missing opportunities. If you're focusing with real clear attention to the moment at hand, it tends to seed the future.

Jim Davis

Occupation: Cartoonist—Creator of Garfield and President of Paws, Inc.

Website: *www.Garfield.com*

Background

Each day, for more than 20 years, in excess of 263 million readers have seen the comical exploits of Garfield—one of the most popular comic strip characters in the world. Because Garfield is translated into 26 languages, cartoonist Jim Davis's wisecracking feline friend refrains from social or political comment, plus never uses rhyming gags, plays on words, or colloquialisms in order convey humor to his worldwide audience. Yet each day's comic strip always offers something new, thanks in large part to Jim's creativity and ability to brainstorm.

Aside from the comic strip, Garfield has been featured in his own animated TV series, starred in 13 prime-time television specials, is the focus of many best-selling books, and can be seen on a plethora of licensed merchandise that is currently sold in 69 countries.

While many would say that Jim created Garfield and controls his character, as you'll soon discover, Jim has a very different philosophy. Although Jim grew up on a farm in Indiana, his asthma kept him from being highly involved with maintaining the farm and caring for the animals (which included 25 cats). Instead, Jim recalls spending hours each day drawing—staying occupied and entertained with little more than pencils and paper.

After college, Jim spent two years working for an advertising agency, but soon met up with cartoonist Tom Ryan, the creator of *Tumbleweeds*. Starting in 1969, he began working as Ryan's assistant. It was a business partnership that lasted for nine years. Most impor-

Jim Davis and his cartoon companions
Garfield and Odie

tantly, it was during this period that Jim obtained the valuable hands-on training that he needed to perfect his skills as an artist and cartoonist.

Back then, even though the world was full of cat lovers, Jim noticed that few comic strips starred cats. Garfield made his newspaper debut shortly thereafter, on June 19, 1978. Together Jim and Garfield have won numerous awards for their work and have achieved incredible success. Appearing in more than 2,500 newspapers everyday, Garfield is the most widely read comic strip in the world.

(Some information within the previous section is from press material provided courtesy of the associated individual or company.)

Interview With Jim Davis

Q: What made you get started as a cartoonist?

JD: It was an opportunity to express myself. I loved to draw, but I wasn't too good at it as a child, so I'd add words to my drawings to make them funny. For example, I'd draw a cow, which didn't look too much like a cow, so I'd write the word *cow* above it and draw an arrow toward my cow drawing. Early on, the concept of putting words with pictures came to me very naturally. I was always able to crack my mom up with my funny drawings. Other people write, act, or dance, for example. For me, drawing cartoons was my form of expression. It's something I've always done without too much conscious thought. I never dreamed I'd earn a living doing this. It was while working for Tom Ryan that I developed the confidence to pursue drawing my own comic feature.

Q: As you were growing up, did you pursue any training to enhance your creativity?

JD: No. My creativity has always been a part of me. Acquiring my artistic skills was a challenge and something I worked hard to obtain. My writing skill, however, comes from somewhere in the deep recesses of my subconsciousness. Another natural ability I have is that I know and understand what makes other people laugh. I've always been fascinated by what entertains people.

Q: Where do your ideas come from, especially when you're working with Garfield?

JD: Part of the process involves me going into a kind of meditation. It's only while I am in this meditative state that I am the most creative and able to brainstorm. I only do a few things consciously to prepare for a brainstorming session. Once the process begins, I watch what happens in my head.

I know Garfield. I can see and hear him in my head. For me, he's alive. All I do consciously when I write is put Garfield in a situation. I then watch what happens within my mind. When Garfield starts moving, I start taking notes to record the ideas. When Garfield does something funny in my mind, I back up three frames and cut it off, then I edit. I can spot a funny gag when I see and hear it taking place in my head. When something cracks me up, I quickly transcribe it onto paper using a combination of text and sketches. Whenever Garfield makes me laugh, it's always with a fresh thought. I never put words in his mouth or force scenarios to happen.

Q: Is there a preset time in your schedule when you brainstorm new ideas?

JD: Yes. I write about one week out of the month. During that week, I will create a month's worth of gags. When I'm in my meditative state, while brainstorming, I can't be distracted by anything else. Usually, the room is quiet. To prepare, I'll sometimes read a funny book or watch a funny TV show the night before I know I'm going to brainstorm.

I always brainstorm at my desk in my office. Typically, I work alone, but I sometimes work with my assistant. The only time I use music in the background for inspiration is when I am working on strips for the holiday season. It could be in July when I'm creating the Garfield strips that will run around Christmas. I will listen to the Johnny Mathis Christmas album to get into the Christmas spirit. Other times during the year, I don't use music for inspiration.

Q: What do you notice about yourself when you're brainstorming?

JD: My mind and body work differently when I am in my meditative state and creating. I was once tested and they determined that my heart rate goes up dramatically when I am creating. When I'm really involved in my writing, I sometimes break out in a sweat and start tapping my foot. This is when I am really focused.

My brainstorming efforts involve using a pad and pens to record my ideas. I also stare a lot at the walls or play with the various toys that surround me. On my desk are funny items, like pig noses, fuzzy hats, and noisemakers. I'm 57-years-old, but when I am creating, I still play with toys when I need inspiration. I have this big rubber spider on my desk, for example. I call him the "funny idea spider." When I think of something funny, I hit him on the head. I use these items to mentally take me away from where I am.

Toys and funny hats inspire Jim's creativity

I know some cartoonists start with a punch line and work backwards when they create. I don't do that. When I am in my meditative state, I see and hear everything Garfield does. Everything else just happens. I don't fully understand how or why it works. The rules I have about not using rhyming gags or plays on words, for example, don't even occur to me. I just go into a place in my mind where these things don't exist. In my mind, I may see 10 gags, but I'll only write down and go forward with one. I automatically do a lot of editing in my head.

Sometimes a gag will come into my head, but later I won't move forward with it for whatever reason. There are times it's because of a play on words that I know won't translate well into other languages. I know people laugh as easily in Tokyo as they do in America. I try to use the gags that I know will make everyone laugh. It's a subconscious decision about what gags I write down and which I don't when I am meditating.

I usually like to add an element of surprise when it comes to conveying the punch line of a gag. There's often some left turn in the last frame of a strip that will make people laugh. My comic strips typically follow a rhythm. I set it up, twist it, and revolve it. I never worry about the vocabulary or sophistication in a gag. The stuff Garfield does is funny, whether someone is 9 or 90.

Q: **When you sit down to brainstorm new ideas for Garfield, what's the biggest challenge you face?**

JD: The challenge is achieving the state of mind where Garfield will start performing for me in my head. Sometimes, he'll just sit there and stare back at me, like he's waiting for something. That's when I'll go outside and work in my garden or do something else for a while. Garfield will usually start performing for me within a few minutes. Sometimes, the process takes and hour or two to begin. Once he starts performing, I have to be ready, because I have to write very quickly, while in my meditative state.

There are times when Garfield will string four, five, or six usable gags together and I'll have to get them all down. Other times, the gags will come, one at a time, about 30 minutes apart. I never know what to expect. When I am really rested and in a great mood, the process works faster and is easier.

For me, during this process, the toughest part is sitting down with a blank sheet of paper in front of me and getting things going. It's not something I can force to happen, but when I'm there, I know it.

Q: **When you're staring at that blank sheet of paper, what's the first step when you brainstorm?**

JD: The first thing I do consciously is put Garfield in a specific situation. I may place him up a tree or watching TV, for example. I then sit back, enter into my meditative state and let Garfield do rest. I play a lot of "what if" games when creating situations in order to generate new ideas. I'll typically come up with a scenario and see how it plays out. If nothing happens, I'll try something else. It's actually Garfield who decides what other characters he'll interact with. Sometimes he'll introduce new characters I don't even know. I can't force a new character into a scenario. This aspect in my work takes place almost on a subconscious level.

Q: **When you're working on a comic strip, how do you know when it's finished?**

JD: It just comes together. The idea for a gag comes to me during my meditative state. I'll sketch it out and takes notes during this process. I'll then go back and do a rough draft of the strip. It later goes next door for the finishing pencil and ink process. When it comes back to me, I'll proof read it, add last minute touches, sign it, and send it out. Rarely, like three or four times in the last 20 years, have I looked at a final strip and scrapped it. Either the art didn't support the gag or something transpired in the meantime that no longer made the gag appropriate.

Q: After so many years, how do you keep your ideas fresh and creative?

JD: I work about one year in advance. Thus, I can move the order of finished strips around before people read them. This helps to keeps things unpredictable. If Garfield is able to make me laugh when I see a gag in my mind, it's something that I've never seen before. Therefore, it's a new and original idea. Those are the ideas I go with. Garfield is always going to be hungry and sleepy. I look for the new twists to these and other scenarios.

Q: Do ideas for gags ever come to you when you're not in your meditative state?

JD: Never. I have to be totally focused on it for the ideas to come to me. I have to go find them. They don't randomly find me.

Q: How can other people learn how to tap into their creativity?

JD: The way I look at it, creativity and brainstorming takes a lot of preparation. The first step to being creative is to learn absolutely everything about your subject matter. Only then can you leap into the unknown. If you're brainstorming about something you don't understand, you'll just be leaping into the known, and that's not creative. Experience certainly counts for something.

When you decide to try creative thinking or brainstorming, know what you're trying to accomplish. You can call this problem solving or whatever you want. You also need to have faith in yourself and the willingness to turn everything over in your mind to develop new ideas. This sometimes takes tremendous effort. I think brainstorming is about one percent inspiration and 99 percent perspiration.

The best results will be generated when you learn everything possible about the subject matter as part of your preparation. It's also extremely helpful to be very excited about what you're doing. This will help you put forth the necessary effort.

Once you start generating ideas, you'll be excited by the reward. There's no greater feeling than coming up with great ideas. When I brainstorm, I always like to consider, in advance, the limitations I have to deal with. For example, if I need to create a cover for a new Garfield book, the publisher might tell me I can only work with two colors, the image must be a specific size, and the production budget must stay very low. I look at limitations as a positive challenge. If there were no limitations, there'd be no need for creativity.

Q: **What do you think holds people back from being creative thinkers?**

JD: Fear of failure. If someone fails at work, that could translate into a loss of their job. This causes fear. People also hate to be wrong. To be a creative thinker, you need to throw caution into the wind and trust your instincts.

When you have a vision for something and you trust that vision, pursue it, even if nobody else sees it the way you do. If you come up with a truly unique idea, there may be nothing to compare it to. Thus, until you try implementing the idea, it's impossible to predict how it will turn out. You need to lose the fear of failure and develop a confidence in yourself. If you're truly creative, along the way you'll think up some really dumb things before that brilliant idea strikes. There's an old saying that you need to kiss a lot of frogs before you find a prince.

Charles Fazzino

Occupation: Artist

Website: *www.fazzino.com*

Background

Charles Fazzino is the most popular 3-D artist in the world today. With over 600 galleries marketing his pieces, he has gathered a loyal following not only in the United States, but throughout Asia, Europe, Australia, and even in South Africa.

As the creator of limited edition fine art silkscreen serigraphs, he is best known for his use of vibrant colors, exceptional detail, and brilliant storytelling ability. It takes a familiarity with Charles Fazzino's artistic process to truly appreciate the talent, effort, and workmanship that goes into creating each edition of art. After going through a hand-printed silkscreen process, each image is meticulously cut, glued, glittered, and assembled, all by hand. Each piece is an individual creation.

Over the course of his 20-year career, Charles Fazzino's popularity has soared. He appears at more than 40 one-man exhibitions and shows annually, treating thousands of fans to his one-of-a-kind signature drawings.

Each year, Fazzino creates 20 to 30 new editions. He is best known for his colorful renditions of New York City, however, he has also immortalized locales such as San Francisco, Jerusalem, Munich, and Atlanta, pop icons such as Marilyn Monroe, Elvis Presley, and the characters of Walt Disney, and famous sports franchises like the New York Yankees, Miami Dolphins, and Denver Broncos.

When asked to describe what he does as an artist, Fazzino refers to his work as "pop art." In this interview, you'll learn what inspires his work and how Fazzino has learned to harness his creativity as an artist to achieve worldwide success and recognition. If you're not familiar with Fazzino's work, be sure to visit his Website to see samples of the three-dimensional pieces he so brilliantly creates.

(Some information within the previous section is from press material provided courtesy of the associated individual or company.)

Charles Fazzino at work

Interview With Charles Fazzino

Q: **What made you decide to become an artist?**

CF: I come from a very artistic family. My mother was a crafter and painter. Back in the 1970s, she did a lot of the outdoor art shows. My father was a women's shoe designer. I grew up around artistic people. There was a lot of creativity in my home. I was influenced at a young age and it became a part of me.

Q: **When did you discover you were truly talented as an artist?**

CF: Back in high school, a lot of my friends were extremely talented in painting and drawing, for example, but I don't recall having that talent. I was not the best artist or best portrait painter. I discovered then that what I possessed were good ideas. Over time, I learned how to conceptualize my ideas and help them evolve. I was able to look at something artistically and package it.

Q: How do you describe or categorize your artwork?

CF: I started off as an illustrator and painter. This is the type of work I did throughout art school. What I do today has developed into this style that has a life of its own. It's very strange. Over time, I have adapted my painting style and started creating what the art circles call three-dimensional "pop art." My artwork has gone through a metamorphosis in terms of its look. These days, I call my art "three-dimensional constructions."

Q: Over the years, what have you done to develop your creativity?

CF: I am constantly trying new things. I challenge myself to do new styles of artwork using different themes. I like to constantly change the look of my work so it never gets stale. I think this ongoing personal challenge forces me to enhance my creativity.

Q: What continues to inspire you and your work?

CF: I love what I do. That's the most important inspiration. One thing I learned from Walt Disney is to find an idea and stick with it. I was an average painter, but when I started mixing my painting style with a three-dimensional look, I discovered something that worked very well when two art forms were married together. These days, my ideas come from my personal experiences and my travels. A lot of my pieces are architecturally based or theme-based around places I've been.

In a "New York State of Mind."

Q: **Once the idea for a piece comes to you, what is your process for transforming that idea into artwork?**

CF: When I am developing a themed piece based on a city, such as New York, Las Vegas—or more recently, Boston—the images and themes that appear in my work are usually based upon exactly where I went, where I stayed, and what I did in that city. If someone looks at my Boston-themed piece, for example, I want that experience to trigger a nostalgic thought about their own visit to Boston.

Q: **When you're developing ideas for a new piece, do you solicit ideas from other people?**

CF: Sometimes I do. I have other artists who work in my studio that I turn to for advice, for example. I also sometimes get suggestions from people at galleries that showcase my work. When I obtain ideas, I don't have any specific formula for determining what advice I utilize. I do, however, go through this thing in my head where I try to determine what will and won't work.

Q: **Do you have a preferred environment in which you like to work when you're creating new artwork?**

CF: I like to work in my studio. I always have jazz music playing in the background. I find that fast pop music will cause me to work faster, so when I'm under a tight deadline, I select music with a faster beat. I am very influenced by music. My studio also has a lot of history, which makes me comfortable when I work there. It is in an old building, which inspires my creativity. Much of my work is done within my studio, however, as I begin to work on each piece that's themed around a city, for example, I'll often take pictures and make my own videotapes of the city, plus make on-location drawings and sketches.

Q: **When you're brainstorming for a new project, what tools do you use?**

CF: I collect all kinds of things and create a lot of sketches. It is often the items that I collect that allow me to recreate the essence of a location. I always carry around a sketchbook and a camera with me, especially when I'm traveling. There have been times, however, when I'll sketch out ideas on random scraps of paper. I remember I was working on a piece with a wedding theme and an idea came to me in the middle of the night. I sketched out the idea on a paper napkin.

Q: **What are the stages, from start to finish, your artwork goes through?**

CF: Each piece starts off as a pencil drawing. Then it progresses into a finished painting. A three-dimensional prototype is then created. From there, we go to the printing process. The whole process takes about six months, and at each stage, the piece often goes through changes as it evolves into the final artwork.

Q: **Some of your art is based around well-known Disney characters, for example. Is it easier for you to build upon existing ideas or create new ideas from scratch?**

CF: As an artist, when I am building my work around an existing idea, such as Mickey Mouse, for example, my hands are tied in a way. The Walt Disney Company has a certain look for a character like Mickey Mouse, and as an artist, I am required to work within the essence of that vision. That gives me less creative license.

Q: **How do you deal with deadlines and pressure?**

CF: I rely on the large group of people who work with me. I try to see myself as a businessperson as well as an artist, but there are times when I rely on my staff. I am unusual in that I am very deadline-oriented. This is an unusual personality trait for an artist to possess. When I am working under pressure, a tight deadline can sometimes be uncomfortable. Some people think my work suffers when I am working under a tight deadline, while others think my work comes out better.

Q: **How do you judge if your ideas and your work are good or bad as you're working?**

CF: That's a hard question. I have done many pieces that I felt strongly about and that I thought were going turn to out to be my best work. When some of those pieces were completed, however, I wasn't happy with them and they weren't as successful as my other pieces. There have also been pieces that I started off not too excited about that turned out incredibly well. I wish I could say that I've learned from all of my mistakes. I try to avoid repeating the same mistakes, but I can't say that I have truly learned from every mistake I have made.

Q: **When someone is involved in a brainstorming session, it is possible to do it wrong?**

CF: As long as you're generating ideas, you aren't doing it wrong. Part of brainstorming involves coming up with bad ideas or ideas that won't achieve your objective. You'll know, however, when the right idea comes along. You can't fear rejection or fear that you won't be able to do something. Fear will hold you back and stunt your creativity. You can't listen to people who dismiss your ideas. You can't be ashamed of your ideas.

Q: **What is the biggest challenge for you when you're actually creating a new piece?**

CF: When I do my in-person signings at galleries, instead of just autographing the artwork someone purchases, I always create some type of original drawing or doodle for them. I started doing this many years ago. Sometimes, the biggest challenge is creating original and personalized sketches or doodles for someone, while they're watching me work during a gallery show. People will sometimes ask for something very specific, and I'm forced to create something on the spot. That's a tremendous amount of pressure, but it has also helped me hone my creative skills as an artist.

Q: **Do you ever experience the artist's equivalent to writer's block? If so, how do you overcome it?**

CF: This has happened many times over the years. I always force myself to put something on paper, no matter what. Staring at a blank piece of paper is a horrible feeling for an artist. I always put something down on that paper and then slowly start to build upon it. Once something it put on the paper, I keep working at it until it evolves into something I am comfortable with. Sometimes this happens quickly, but not always. There have been times when I will actually go back to completed pieces and rework them later.

Q: **When you're working on a piece of artwork, how do you know when it's completed?**

CF: When the deadline for it to go to the printer comes around. I am sometimes putting last minute touches on pieces less than an hour before it has to be shipped out. I always try to be objective about my work, but sometimes that's hard.

Q: **Outside of creating artwork, how does your creativity impact your life?**

CF: My creativity plays a role in how I conduct and manage my business. It also influences how I deal with people. There's a whole creative flow involved with how you successfully deal with people in personal and business situations.

Q: **What advice do you have for someone first learning how to brainstorm and tap into their creativity?**

CF: I think part of being successful is finding something that you really enjoy, and then you need to keep doing it. Nothing comes easily, without hard work and practice. You have to be persistent. Never say no. Constantly try to assert yourself and keep going. You must keep pushing yourself. I believe everyone has some level of creativity within them. Many people just haven't developed their creativity or learned how to access it yet. To be extremely successful and very creative, I think it may require some positive creative influence at an early age. Some of it might also be genetic. I'm not sure. When someone needs to be creative, but the ideas aren't coming to them, the easiest thing to do is quit. That's what most people do. The trick is to be persistent. Never say you can't do something, especially if it's something you really want to do.

Q: Do you have any other advice?

CF: Everything starts with a small idea that evolves into a greater idea. If you're a businessperson who needs or wants to enhance your creativity to become more successful, you might consider taking some type of art class, simply as a creative exercise. Also, being around other people who can help you develop upon or expand your ideas is always a positive influence.

Ferras

Occupation: Singer/Songwriter/Pianist

Website: *www.FerrasMusic.com*

20-year-old performing artist Ferras

Background

When it comes to art, few people have touched the hearts of so many like Picasso. In the world of theater, it's William Shakespeare who has captured people's imaginations for generations. Musically, people like Elton John, Andrew Lloyd Webber, and Billy Joel have demonstrated a natural ability to reach into people's souls as they share their music with the world.

Out of all the people in the world who call themselves artists, few are truly born to perform and have the natural talent to win over audiences of all ages and from all walks of life. At the age of 20, Ferras is one such person. Now stepping onto the music scene, he is a young performer, songwriter, and pianist whose natural abilities transcend any specific writing style and whose looks and stage presence captivate every audience he performs for.

Whether performing original pop music that's accompanied by the type of upbeat and hard-hitting choreography one expects from Britney Spears, or sitting alone in front of a piano performing an original ballad that's as heart wrenching, meaningful, and powerful as any Whitney Houston or Barbara Streisand performance, Ferras is quickly proving he's destined for superstardom in the music industry.

Performing his own material, Ferras doesn't just entertain his audiences—he inspires them with meaningful lyrics, memorable melodies, and an emotional intensity that simply can't be forgotten or ignored. While some musicians spend the greater part of their lives training their voice and mastering their craft, Ferras's talents are self-taught and natural. His unique writing style, image, and stage presence are truly his own.

Ferras's musical influences come from everywhere. Yet what's in this young performer's heart and what he offers in his music are clearly what appeals to his mass-market audience—typically comprised of an extremely broad demographic of males and females, teens and adults alike.

While growing up, Ferras has faced many challenges beyond what's normal for a typical teen. Having overcome every personal and professional obstacle ever placed in his path, it continues to be these traumatic and sometimes heart-wrenching experiences that inspire his music.

While winning over the hearts of America's demanding teenagers with his heartthrob-like appearance, talents, and personality, Ferras is also capturing the attention of music industry professionals and other current chart-topping artists, both as a performer and songwriter. "It's what I was born to do!" he says with a conviction that one can't help but totally believe.

As you're about to discover, Ferras is a musical prodigy with a tremendous amount of creativity and talent that will inspire just about anyone. To hear some of his original music firsthand, be sure to visit his Website at *www.FerrasMusic.com.*

Interview With Ferras

Q; When did you know you had the creative talent and natural ability to be a musician?

F: When I was 5 years old, I was in a restaurant with my parents. There was a piano player performing. When I got home, I sat down at a little toy keyboard and started playing the exact music I heard at the restaurant. To this day, I have never had any music training whatsoever. From that moment, I became very familiar with music and discovered I could play anything I heard. A few years later, I started writing and performing my own music on the piano, which later developed into writing songs with lyrics.

Q: **Without any formal music training, what have you done to perfect your musical abilities and enhance your creativity?**

F: I practice! I play the piano and sing up to six hour per day. I play music and write music. I am always performing and playing. It's an innate ability that comes from somewhere inside me. I am constantly teaching myself different ways of expressing my music. I am always looking to be inundated with sounds. I also look to a lot of the great musicians and composers for inspiration. I derive inspiration, motivation, and ideas from everything that happens to me and that's around me.

Music, in one form or another, is constantly running through me. I believe I exist on a vibration of music. Whether or not I am paying attention, I always have some song in my head. When I sit down and play the piano, I am manifesting all of that which has been bouncing around in my head for the past few minutes, hours, or days. Even without a piano in front of me, I am always practicing in my mind and coming up with new ideas.

Q: **Knowing you had the talent to be a singer, pianist, and songwriter, what inspired you to pursue it professionally?**

F: I have always just known what I'm supposed to do with my life. I've always found it fascinating to hear young people say they don't know what to do with their lives. I have always known that I've wanted to be a performer and be in front of people. I am most comfortable when I am on stage, with a piano, performing, or when I am writing music. When I am doing this, I feel like I am fulfilling my life's destiny.

Q: **What keeps you inspired to create new music?**

F: As with anything, there's always a dry spell in my creativity. Sometimes, I go for a few months and don't write anything new. All of a sudden, a storage bank of ideas and inspirations inside me will unlock and I'll write several new songs in a very short time. This typically happens at the most random times. All of these pent up thoughts and emotions will just pour out of me in the form of music and lyrics. My ideas and inspirations are almost always based upon feelings, emotions, personal experiences, or things I see firsthand. I could be driving and get a tune or melody in my head. After a few minutes, I'll start singing along to it.

Q: **Does all of your music tend to be autobiographical and focus on negative experiences from your life?**

F: Usually, but not always. All of my experiences, including those that could easily be looked at in a negative way, have helped me grow emotionally and mentally. If I could take back some of the things I have experienced or some of the things that have happened to me, I probably would. At the same time, I am grateful, because I am 20 years old, and I know that a lot of my experiences have helped me get to this point in my life. I feel very evolved as a human being. I know that if it weren't for some of the negative experiences in my life, I would not be where I am today.

Q: **How do you brainstorm when you're writing music? What process do you go through?**

F: I will always start by creating the tune. Sometimes I will get so engulfed by the music, it will totally take me away. It's like there's no more Ferras. It almost comes from a source outside of me. That's where the music comes from. I can't really explain that. I will be sitting at the piano and the music will come. As for the lyrics, those come to me based on something that has happened to me that day or from thoughts going through my head. Sometimes, it's the tone of the music that helps the lyrics form in my head. If it's a somber melody or an upbeat melody, that will also have a huge influence on the lyrics I create. A lot depends on my emotional state and the mood I'm in when I am composing.

Ferras

Typically, it all starts with a melody or tune. The tune creates the mood and the mood I'm in creates the lyrics. When you collectively look at it, it eventually becomes a song.

Q: When you sit down to write a song, do you always start with a goal or objective?

F: No. Most of the time, I'll just sit down at the piano, because that's my personal form of meditation. It's how I relax and it's what makes me happy. When I am playing music, it doesn't feel like I am spending time doing something. It's just a natural instinct for me to go to the piano and start creating music.

Sometimes, however, I'll sit down with the intention of writing a specific type of song. In this situation, I'll spend time brainstorming and bouncing around ideas for a melody and lyrics I think could be commercially viable or that people would enjoy listening to.

Q: As you're composing new music and lyrics, how do you evaluate your own work? Are you critical of yourself?

F: I am extremely critical of my work. I think everyone is their own worst critic, including myself. Usually, after the song is finished, I go through it and figure out if it works or not. Some songs could be commercially successful. Others are more live performance pieces, and some will never be heard by others. When I have a specific goal in mind for a song, I want it to be absolutely perfect.

As I said earlier, the music tends to come together by itself. It's the foundation for the song. The lyrics are often what require many revisions and a lot of tinkering before they're ready to be heard by others.

Q: Do you have a perfect environment to work in when you're composing or practicing?

F: Yes. I like to be alone, in a room with lots of windows and a piano. I like to have the lights dim, a cup of hot tea nearby, and a lot of candles lit. Candlelight is very inspiring to me. I usually create my best music late at night. This type of environment tends to make me the most open minded and comfortable, but I don't require it to be creative.

Sometimes, inspiration comes to me at the strangest times. I wrote one of my favorite songs in the lobby of a courthouse. I was there paying a parking ticket. I wound up sitting down in the courtyard of this courthouse and writing a song. Having grown up in Santa Barbara, California, the ocean has also been a part of my life. It truly inspires me.

Q: Aside from a piano, do you use any tools to help you brainstorm?

F: Not really. I always have a pen and paper on hand to write down ideas as they come to me. Other than that, it's just my mind and the piano.

Q: When you're being creative, it is easier or harder to work under pressure, such as when you have a tight deadline?

F: It's not easier or harder. It's a totally different type of creative process for me. If someone gives me a deadline to write a song in three days, for example, I'll start off super charged up and spend a lot of time on it, but then I'll need to take a day off and return to it on the third day. I tend to work well under pressure. I don't think, however, deadlines are particularly helpful when trying to be creative. Creativity is a process that happens at its own pace. I don't think it's possible to consciously sit down and say, "Okay, I am going to be creative right now." It's a natural process. I know when I am working under a deadline, I am more focused. It's a different mindset.

Q: How do you judge your work as you're composing?

F: I listen to a lot of music and I follow pop culture extremely closely. I think I am a good judge of what people enjoy. Having a thorough understanding of my intended audience is important for creating music that will appeal to them. Deep down, I typically know when something I create is excellent, good, or just okay. I have come to trust my own instincts and I rely heavily on them. I also have a close-knit circle of people with whom I share all of my stuff, in order to get their feedback. I know these people will be brutally honest with me.

Q: What are some of the most rewarding experiences you've had thus far?

F: There have been a few instances when I have gotten extremely positive feedback from some of the biggest and most successful people in the recording industry, in terms of other artists, producers, and record label executives. It's that validation, from people I consider to be music legends, that has been extremely rewarding for me. Of course, when I perform in public and see people's reactions to my music firsthand, or when I receive positive e-mails from people who have heard my songs, that's also an incredible feeling.

Q: For you, what is the biggest challenge you face when tapping into your creativity to compose music?

F: Without a doubt, I'd have to say that the biggest challenge is to be fearless. To create music that's based on my own experiences and emotions, I have to allow myself to be extremely vulnerable. A lot of time, people are held back when they feel like they're going to be judged, especially when it relates to some form of art. I think the biggest challenge is being brave enough to take risks from a creative standpoint. It's the people who are fearless and who make themselves vulnerable who are successful, because they're giving the outside world a glimpse into their soul. As an artist, I need to allow myself to be judged and criticized for my work, yet no matter what feedback I receive, I still need to go forth in the way I see fit.

Many of my songs are extremely personal and very emotional, but I don't think there's anything I have ever been too scared to share in my music. Like anyone else, I want privacy in certain aspects of my life, but I believe it's my purpose in life to share my music, which also means sharing very personal aspects of my life. I have never been afraid to show my emotions, especially through my music. People appreciate intimacy and honesty. It's what makes my music appealing and real.

Q: **When you're writing a song or engaged in a brainstorming session, how do you know when you're done?**

F: You just know when the right set of ideas and inspirations have come to you. When you look at the finished product, in my case, a song, you know in your heart that you've finished and that it's ready to be shared. It's very easy to overanalyze something to the point where you never complete it. I simply trust my instincts.

Q: **What advice do you have for someone looking to enhance their own creativity and brainstorming skills?**

F: Be fearless! Everybody has the ability to be creative and to be a great thinker. I believe people have different mediums for expressing their creativity. One way to enhance your creativity is to experience new things and to take yourself out of your ordinary surroundings. Travel, do and see new things, and discover what inspires you. You need to consciously make the decision to not allow yourself to be closed-minded. The first step is to want to open your mind and progress. Once you have the willingness and the drive to expand mentally and creatively, that's when you need to experience things that you normally wouldn't."

CHAPTER 11

Brainstorming Success Stories From the Business World

The interviews you're about to read are with entrepreneurs and business people, from corporate America, who excel at what they do. Each person featured within this chapter credits at least some of their success directly to their ability to brainstorm and think creatively, even in situations when they're surrounded by analytical thinkers.

Each of these people has a very different background and set of job responsibilities, yet each discovered how being a creative thinker can be extremely beneficial in their day-to-day work. As you read the interviews, even if you have nothing in common from a career standpoint with the people you're reading about, consider adapting the advice that's offered into your own life and learn from the firsthand experiences of these people.

These people have already discovered how to brainstorm and think creatively. They have successfully adopted these skills into their work, and they have achieved documented results that you could possibly replicate by adopting the same strategies into your life.

Jim McCann

Title: Founder & CEO

Company: 1-800-Flowers.com

Website: *www.1800Flowers.com*

Background

Sometimes brainstorming leads to such a good idea that people are willing to take tremendous risks in order to see their idea become a reality. Years ago, while working as a social worker, Jim McCann developed the idea to open a single florist shop. He quit his stable job, invested every penny he had, and opened his small business.

It wasn't long, however, before his next big idea came along. He wanted to acquire the toll-free phone number 1-800-Flowers and begin taking flower orders over the telephone. This was at a time when toll-free numbers were not commonplace and few consumers placed orders for anything over the

Jim McCann, founder and CEO of
1-800-FLOWERS.com

telephone. He wound up having to purchase a failing company that owned the phone number, into which he again invested every penny he had, and transform that business into a profitable venture.

Although Jim refuses to acknowledge that he's a creative person, throughout his careers, he's generated and implemented many unique and potentially risky ideas, which have lead to one success after another. Today 1-800-Flowers owns and operates a successful chain of over 120 retail florists, the toll-free 1-800-Flowers phone number, and 1800-Flowers.com—which has become one of the most successful online businesses in the world. The company has also expanded into other industries, for example, by acquiring the Plow and Hearth mail-order company (*www.plowhearth.com*) and Magic Cabin Dolls (*www.magiccabindolls.com*).

As you're about to discover, under the leadership of Jim McCann, Westbury, New York-based 1-800-Flowers.com is a business that thrives on creativity and innovative thinking.

(Some information within the previous section is from press material provided courtesy of the associated individual or company.)

Interview With Jim McCann

Q: **What inspires your creative thinking and brainstorming abilities?**

JM: To tell you the truth, I am not a revolutionary or creative thinker. To illustrate my point, there was once a judge who was asked to define pornography. He responded, "I don't know how to define pornography, but I know it when I see it." When it comes to good ideas, I know them when I see them. I am a mimic. I surround myself with talented and bright people. In my life, I have met some extremely interesting and successful people. I've always tried to mimic aspects of those people's behaviors that inspire me. One definition of creativity is taking a great idea from one field and reapplying it into another field. That's what I am good at.

I believe there's no such thing as a new idea. What I do is read extensively and I listen to great speakers. When I come across an idea, I think about how that idea would work in my world or benefit my company. I am not someone who can brainstorm by myself in order to work through a problem. I am not good at that. What I am good at is gathering a group of people with a diverse set of knowledge and skills, and stimulating a dialog that transforms into a productive group brainstorming session.

Q: **At 1-800-Flowers.com, do you host regular brainstorming sessions?**

JM: Yes, but they're not typically that formal. What I strive for is to generate group dialog in a creative environment. Sometimes, this happens over a pizza, after a basketball game, or on a golf course. I always try to get people to talk about ideas and challenge them to be outrageous.

In a group, I will challenge everyone, including someone who is extremely shy in the group, to come up with ideas and discuss them. I will point to someone in a meeting and say to them, "I'm going to come back to you in a few minutes. I want you to have the most outrageous and outlandish idea there is, in regard to what we can do here." The person might spend the next few minutes sweating, turning colors, and being frightened, but when I come back to him or her, they'll almost always have two or three really good ideas that are ready to be shared.

It's amazing the way ideas come about and where they come from. The ideas rarely, if ever, come directly from me. I am usually the catalyst. I can tell a story, craft a vision, and gather people together, but it's those people that typically generate the really good ideas.

Q: **Could you explain your philosophy about how the best ideas come from humor?**

JM: Look at the best business ideas we've seen in our lifetime. The best business ideas started out with people laughing at them. Look at FedEx,

Blockbuster, or Wal-Mart, with its plan to overtake the world with large stores in rural areas. Humor is the key ingredient for creativity. I like to hang around people who have good senses of humor and who see things in a wacky sort of way. My job is to get these people to talk and be outrageous, but not necessarily to solve specific problems.

Q: **Do you always start a brainstorming session with a goal or objective?**

JM: Sometime, but usually not. Some of the best ideas generated in the history of our company came about while eating a pizza at 3:00 a.m., on a Saturday before Mother's Day [one of 1-800-Flowers's busiest holidays], for example. In this situation, I've had people whip out a marker and outline their idea on the back of a pizza box. Once someone starts formulating an idea, I follow up by asking lots of questions.

Q: **Do you utilize any specific tools when brainstorming?**

JM: When we're involved in an organized brainstorming session, we use white boards. I'm also a list-maker.

Q: **During or after a brainstorming session, how do you evaluate ideas?**

JM: I don't have a clearly defined set of rules for this. Criteria I use involves determining if the idea is newsworthy. 1-800-Flowers.com is a very public relations-driven company. I ask, if we pursued a new idea, would journalists write about it?

You can't be afraid to make mistakes. I have made dozens of mistakes. If you're not making mistakes, I believe you're not trying hard enough.

Q: **Have you ever pursued a bad idea? If so, what did you learn from it?**

JM: Almost every day! One of the biggest mistakes of my life was buying the 1-800-Flowers company. This could have become the biggest disaster in my life, but at the time, I was too stupid to lie down and give up. People laughed at us when we got started.

I remember traveling on an airplane and sitting next to someone in the oil business. He asked me what I did, and I told him I was in the flower business and owned a company called "1-800-Flowers." He looked at me with a confused expression and asked why I didn't call the company "799-Flowers," because he had no clue what an 800-telephone number was. It was at that moment that I knew we had a huge task ahead of us in terms of educating the customers, not just about our company, but also about how to use a toll-free phone number to place an order for something. At the time, this was a revolutionary idea. I was personally on the hook for the almost $10-million investment needed to buy the then Dallas-based 1-800-Flowers business, which was initially a huge failure.

I thought buying that company was a good idea. It turned out initially to be a terrible idea. However, I refused to quit. I am like an ant. I keep building the anthill. Sometimes, the best ideas take a crazy person to keep pushing them. These are some of the lessons I've learned.

Q: **1-800-Flowers has always been one step ahead in terms of trends. For example, you are a industry leader in e-commerce, and you helped establish using toll-free phone numbers in business. Is being a creative thinker in the business world the same as being able to accurately predict future trends?**

JM: No. These are different concepts. I think we can all figure out what's coming if we spend the time to actually look. About 15 years ago, I remember spending time with the president of Fidelity Investments. At the time, the company was created with the premise that all communication with clients could be done over the telephone. Yet Fidelity was in the process of opening many retail store locations. I inquired about this, because it didn't make sense to me.

I learned from Fidelity that customers felt more comfortable doing their investment work over the telephone, but wanted the peace of mind knowing that if something went wrong, they could show up in person and get face-to-face help. Thus, Fidelity opened retail stores, not to generate more business, but to give its customers peace of mind.

This was a lesson I've been mimicking ever since. 1-800-Flowers is a multichannel retailer with a chain of retail stores, even though our primary business is the toll-free phone number and the Website. Having the retail stores gives us credibility and additional marketing muscle. We're not just your local florist. We're your floral and gift company. You can drive by one of our stores or see our logoed trucks driving around in your community, which helps in a subtle way to paint that picture.

Q: **Once you come up with a great idea, how do you decide the best way to proceed and implement that idea?**

JM: I usually paint the picture for the idea and turn it over to someone else, with the directive to take the idea and make it bigger. For example, we have a totally new brand within the company which launched October 1, 2002. Once the idea was generated, I took a bright and aggressive young man and woman who worked for us and made it their project. I gave them 60 days to develop the business. I gave them the idea and the resources to make it happen. The rest was up to them.

Everyday I ran into these two people, I used humor to motivate them. I'd say things like, "I'm nervous you're going to run us out of business."

or "What? You need a 30-day extension? I thought you were good at what you do!" I used a lot of humor to challenge them.

Generally, this approach works. Sometimes, the person I assign a project to doesn't have what it takes to implement it properly. I figure that if we achieve great success one out of 10 times, that's a good hit ratio.

Once I turn an idea over to someone, they own it. It becomes their baby. If nobody owns an idea or project, nothing will get done.

Q: Once you utilize your creative team to generate ideas, do you turn over the implementation of those ideas to more analytical thinkers?

JM: I don't make that distinction. I have pulled accountants into brainstorming sessions, for example, and their creative input has been extremely helpful.

I read a lot. I will often tear articles out of magazines and use a marker to circle a key idea that somehow relates to my company. I'll then forward that article to someone within the company with a memo stating, "This is how this company is handling the issue. What relevancy does it have to us and our strategy?" I encourage them to think about it for a few days and then get back to me with three or four bullet points about how the idea in the article could be utilized by us. I constantly use ideas from other fields to challenge people from our company.

Q: What is the biggest challenge you and your employees face when trying to tap into your creativity?

JM: We need to avoid thinking, "Oh my God, I need to tap into my creativity!" To overcome this, I use a lot of "what if" and "why not" questions to get people thinking in a creative way. I also get people to start off with their most outrageous ideas and encourage them with humor. There are so many things we always want to do. I have to make sure I am spending my time on the right things in order to generate the best possible results in terms of the big picture. A lot of the time, I find that we are busy, but we're not spending time on the right things to generate the results we want or need. Each person needs to spend the majority of their time on the key three, four, or five projects that will make the most difference.

Q: How do you deal with situations when you want to be creative, but the ideas don't flow? What do you do to get things moving?

JM: I will call on various people I know I work well with, in terms of tapping into our creativity together. I will also go back and do more reading in order to generate inspiration.

Q: **What advice can you offer to someone first learning how to be a creative thinker?**

JM: Take chances! Don't be afraid of looking like an idiot. Don't be afraid to laugh at yourself or have people laugh at your ideas. If people do laugh, you've started down the right path. Laughing has an amazing effect in terms of allowing people to release good energies and positive chemical reactions in the brain. What holds most people back from being good at brainstorming or being creative thinkers are shyness and personal insecurity.

Patti Hill and Andrea Bargsley

Title: Cofounders

Company: BlabberMouth Public Relations

BLaBBeRMouTH

Website: *www.blabbermouth.biz*

Background

Public relations firms exist to help clients utilize the media to generate publicity and improve their public images or reputations. Like advertising agencies, PR firms are typically staffed by groups of extremely creative people. While there are some extremely large and powerful PR firms that represent some of the world's best known companies, there are also smaller firms that specialize in working with smaller clients and implementing more grassroots public relations campaigns.

According to Patti and Andrea, "We are a marketing and public relations agency specializing in branding, creative design, and corporate awareness. We're not your typical marketing firm. At BlabberMouth, we approach marketing and public relations a little differently. We take time to sit down and get to know all about your organization, goals, pitfalls, and needs. We're always looking out for your best interests while compiling clever ways to successfully move your goods and services through the marketing chain."

To achieve this objective, these two partners follow their seven rules of marketing, which are:

1. Find the inherent drama within your offering.

2. Translate that unique quality into a meaningful benefit.

3. State your benefits as believably as possible.

4. Get people's attention.

5. Motivate your audience to do something.

6. Be sure you are communicating clearly.

7. Measure the effectiveness of your campaign.

Throughout this book, you've read about many different ways people brainstorm to achieve success. Patti Hill and Andrea Bargsley operate a relatively new and small public relations firm from a small town in Texas. They're featured in this book not because of the work they do with their clients, but because of the innovative brainstorming technique they utilize whenever they need to tap into their creativity.

Instead of brainstorming in an office conference room or at their desks, these two entrepreneurs hop on their bicycles and set off on 50-mile cross-country treks several times per week, during which they brainstorm. While you might not be an avid bike rider, what you'll learn from this interview is how extensive physical exercise while brainstorming can be a useful tool for your mind and body.

(Some information within the previous section is from press material provided courtesy of the associated individual or company.)

Interview With Patti Hill and Andrea Bargsley

Q: How do you set yourself apart in the PR field?

PH: Both Andrea and I come from the IT [Information Technology] training field. All of the principles we use to help our clients, we also use on ourselves, which is how we attract our new clients. We consider ourselves to really be blabbermouths. I think people see what we've done in terms of promoting ourselves, and they hire us to do it for them as well. Neither one of us has specialized training in marketing or public relations, but we really love what we do, and we are really good at it.

Q: How do you generate your ideas while bike riding for 50 miles at a time?

PH: The bike rides themselves are grueling. After the first hour, the physical exertion leads us to get into a euphoric place where we have a heightened sense of awareness. One of us will think of something and then we start bouncing ideas freely off each other as we ride. It always starts off with casual conversation.

Q: When you embark on a bike ride, is there always a brainstorming objective you start with?

PH: No. The goal is to ride. The ideas are a byproduct. Andrea and I are on the same team from a work standpoint, but we're also in the same mental state as we're riding. This works much better than sitting around in an office, which provides a very stagnant situation. Through bike riding, we are motivating our bodies and, as a result, also motivating our minds.

Q: What is your brainstorming process when biking?

PH: We always plan the dates for our bike trips in advance. We ride about two days per week. We'll put those two dates in our calendar. We don't, however, decide where we're going to ride or the exact distance of the trip until the day before. When the time comes, we head into the country by car to reach our starting location. We have a lot of maps and know many different bike routes. We'll typically ride for several hours. We start off with small talk during the first hour. That gets our minds going.

Q: Did you start bike riding knowing that you'd use it as a brainstorming tool on an ongoing basis?

PH: No. We started doing this as a way to clear our heads and exercise our bodies. When you're working out, on a bike, for example, you get to the point where you don't want to think about your legs going up and down anymore, so you're almost forced to think about something else. Usually, our conversation during the ride will generate one idea that gets built upon as we go. We often become totally consumed with our ideas during the rides and oblivious to what's happening around us.

AB: From the time we started working together, Patti and I figured out that we don't brainstorm well during the day sitting at our desks. Even before we started biking, we'd generate our best ideas in the middle of the night when communicating via e-mail. During the day, when we tried to brainstorm, we had to force the ideas to come, and that never worked for us.

Q: How do you record your ideas if you're riding a bike?

AB: The moment the bike ride ends, we'll both sit down at our computers and type out detailed notes about everything we talked or thought about.

Q: Once you generate your ideas, how do you implement them?

AB: We always start by building a detailed plan around the idea, whether it's for a PR campaign or an event. We'll pass the plan back and forth between us and build upon it. At times, we'll bring in other people as they're needed. From there, we create the project calendar and timeline. After that, we start implementing.

Q: How do you evaluate your ideas once you've come up with them?

AB: We usually move forward with the ideas we're both really excited about. The ideas we're not both sold on we'll discuss, and it'll eventually morph into something else that's completely different and mutually acceptable.

PH: We'll take each idea and try to think of all the things that won't work. We'll then make a list of all the reasons why the idea will work. This allows us to look at the entire picture. Things become pretty obvious from there.

Q: **What's the biggest challenge you face when trying to be creative?**

PH: The biggest challenge is trying to be creative when working under a tight deadline. Because we use project calendars and timelines, we rarely find ourselves way behind. We sometimes take on more work than we feel we can handle, but in those cases, we'll work harder or bring in additional people.

AB: Another challenge is dealing with difficult clients. If we don't totally believe in what the client is trying to do, it's a lot harder to be creative on their behalf. Thus, we make a conscious effort to take on only clients we know we'll work well with. What we do isn't perfect for every potential client. We'll sometimes refer work to other PR firms if we're not comfortable taking on a prospective client.

Q: **Once you come up with an idea for a client, how do you get them to buy into your vision or idea?**

AB: If we're going to pitch an idea to a client, it's already something we're very excited about and believe in. We also become very excited about what our client is doing. We're such outgoing people, our excitement automatically gets transferred over to the client. We never need any visual tools, for example, to communicate an idea. It's just us talking to them. Because we choose clients we know are very excited about what they do, they welcome ideas from people as passionate as they are about their work. We make sure that what we deliver is exactly what they're looking for.

Q: **What advice do you have for someone who wants to become a more creative thinker?**

PH: Try to stay relaxed, at least as far as your mind is concerned. When we're on our bike treks, it's a relaxed atmosphere, even though our bodies are working hard. Andrea and I are competitive enough so we keep each other going, but it's not a stressful situation. Stress kills creativity! Whatever you need to do to eliminate stress, do it. For us, it's riding a bike. For others, it might be to get a massage or participate in some other sport. It also helps to work with people you like and who you get along with. This allows you to work off each other when being creative. We build off of each other's ideas.

Q: **What holds most people back from being creative?**

PH: They start off with the wrong attitude and they're not excited about whatever it is they're trying to do. I read recently that 85 percent of people hate their jobs. That's pitiful. If you're starting off in this mindset, that's a big obstacle you'll need to overcome.

AB: Many people are also afraid to be creative. To practice being creative, try different activities to help you open up. Try a creative writing exercise, but make sure you write about something you're passionate about. It's always a challenging activity to write a creative ad about yourself or someone close to you.

Paul Barker

Title: Senior Vice President

Company: Hallmark Cards, Inc.

Website: *www.Hallmark.com*

Background

Everyday millions of people celebrate special occasions and use Hallmark greeting cards as one way to share a wide range of special sentiments and convey personal messages about such things as love, friendship, sympathy, and excitement.

Hallmark was founded in January 1910 by Joyce C. Hall, who ultimately established the Hallmark brand's reputation for quality through uncompromising attention to detail. Since 1944, Hallmark has used the well-known slogan, "When you care enough to send the very best."

Over the years, Hallmark has achieved distinction through its products, its network of specialty retail stores, national advertising, and as sponsor of the *Hallmark Hall of Fame*—one of television's most honored and enduring dramatic series.

These days, you can find Hallmark cards and other products sold at more than 42,000 retail outlets, domestically. The company also publishes products in more than 30 languages and distributes them in more than 100 countries.

In addition to its flagship brand, Hallmark markets products under the brand names Expressions From Hallmark and Ambassador. Some of the company's other well known product lines include: Hallmark Keepsake Ornaments, Party Express From Hallmark, and Shoebox Greetings. Hallmark's Binney & Smith subsidiary markets products branded Crayola (crayons) and Silly Putty. Meanwhile, Hallmark Entertainment has become the world's

Paul Barker, Senior Vice President of Hallmark, Inc.

leading producer and distributor of miniseries and television movies and oversees the new Hallmark Channel on cable television.

Hallmark is a company that's based upon creativity in everything it does. This creativity has lead to tremendous financial success. In 2001, for example, Hallmark reported consolidated net revenues of $4.0 billion. Hallmark's creative staff consists of more than 1,300 artists, designers, stylists, writers, editors, and photographers. Together they generate more than 23,000 new and redesigned greeting cards and related products per year. The company offers more than 40,000 products at any one time.

Worldwide, Hallmark has more than 20,000 full-time employees. About 5,500 people work at the Kansas City corporate headquarters, including Paul Barker, the company's senior vice president of creativity. Paul personally oversees the entire creative staff. In this interview, he shares his insights about creative thinking and brainstorming.

(Some information within the previous section is from press material provided courtesy of the associated individual or company.)

Interview With Paul Barker

Q: How did you wind up as the executive at Hallmark in charge of the company's entire creative team?

PB: I went to school at the University of Arizona and earned a degree in graphic design and illustration. I started working for Hallmark as an artist 23 years ago. I've also worked as a photographer, designer, illustrator, and as a manager of studio artists. In the past, I have also worked on the business side, running one of Hallmark's business units. I now manage the entire creative organization, comprised of about 1,300 people. We're all targeted and focused on creating compelling products, including greeting cards, ornaments, gifts, gift wrap, and party goods.

Q: **When did you realize you were creative and could utilize your abilities professionally?**

PB: As a very young child, I loved to draw and write. As far back as I can remember, I have always enjoyed expressing my creativity through art. Over the years, in addition to studying art in high school and college, I also studied the sciences and went down the pre-med degree path. Eventually, I had to decide between medicine and art. Ironically, many of the science and math classes have really helped me, not from an artistic perspective, but from a creative problem solving perspective.

A good designer and creative thinker understands the world around them. That's why it is important to have exposure to history, science, math, and economics, for example. This exposure will help someone understand their world and be able to solve problems better because of that understanding.

Q: **What do you see as being your primary goal managing the creative team at Hallmark?**

PB: Our business is all about enhancing and nurturing relationships. We help people say things to other people that they don't know how to say by themselves. People have their feelings and emotions, but sometime need help expressing them when it comes to celebrating birthdays; honoring anniversaries; or experiencing a difficult life change, such as the loss of a loved one. People have their emotions locked up deep inside. Our job within the creative group at Hallmark is to figure out how we can help unlock those feelings and emotions in meaningful and relevant ways. Our job is to brainstorm all of the different ways people can express their feelings in a lighthearted, serious, emotional, and/or humorous way.

Everything we do from a creative standpoint is about enhancing relationships and enriching lives. Thus, we can focus our creative energies toward this, and it's amazing the types of things that result from our endeavors. Relevancy is also important. We don't want to put ideas in people's heads. We want to help them convey what they are already feeling in a way that's appropriate to them personally. In order to cater to everyone, this requires a lot of diversification in what we offer.

Q: **Where do your ideas typically come from in terms of your inspiration?**

PB: All of the creative people at Hallmark, including myself, try to surround ourselves with as much stimuli as possible. We do as much as we can to bring the outside world in. We'll bring in guest speakers. We have a large library. Everyone in the creative community has Internet access at their desk. We follow trends, subscribe to magazines, watch movies, read books, and expose ourselves to everything we think our consumers are exposed to. We also send people out on research trips as well as to our retail stores. The goal is to expose people to as many things as possible, because the creative process never really stops. It goes on 24 hours per day.

All of the input and creative stimuli we're exposed to gets stored somewhere in our brains, so at the right time, it can be pulled out in a creative way as an illustration, photograph, poem, or product idea, for example. When the idea comes out, it's always given some type of personalized twist that makes it unique.

We want to know what makes people happy and sad, and what makes them worried for example. We need to know exactly what's shaping the consumers' emotional lives so we can create the best and most appropriate products possible. It all comes down to knowing our market.

Q: **What is your process for holding brainstorming sessions at Hallmark?**

PB: This varies, depending on what we're trying to accomplish. Sometimes we'll know very specifically what problem we're trying to solve, but not always. Sometimes, our brainstorming is much more open-ended. For example, when we recently started working with poet Dr. Maya Angelou, we knew there was something pretty wonderful there, but we didn't know what the end product was going to be in terms of our collaborative partnership. It was through a number of brainstorming sessions that we decided on the product formats, the messages, the voice, as well as the look and feel of the product line. Sometimes, you don't know what the outcome will be, but you know it should be something pretty wonderful. Other times, you know exactly what the outcome will be, but you don't know how to get there.

I will sometimes create brainstorming teams comprised of a mix of people with very varied backgrounds and talents. I like diversity of thinking when it comes to brainstorming. If we know what we're trying to create and have a defined goal, I might establish a specialized team with very specific skills and knowledge. It all comes down to building a team that I think will generate the results we're striving for.

To inspire people during a brainstorming session, we'll sometimes take a trip to the 80-acre farm that Hallmark owns. It's located about 40 minutes away from our headquarters. This is a retreat that we've created that takes us far away from the corporate environment. Our teams can get away from their day-to-day work, enjoy the lake, and be inspired by the outdoors. We try to employ a variety of means to help us come up with ideas.

Q: How do you describe the perfect brainstorming environment?

PB: We try to be as flexible as we can. It all depends on the situation. One of the things we want to make sure we don't lose is the authenticity of the ideas. We don't want ideas to be forced. If our product ideas, for example, are forced, consumers will sense this and that hurts the company as a whole.

Sometimes, we'll tailor the environment to include music. At times, the environment will be very quiet, while at other times, it will be extremely loud and active. We'll bring in games, watch TV and movies, and participate in fun activities to stimulate people's thinking. There are times, however, when it's like cramming for an exam and the atmosphere is very serious. I believe in customizing the environment specifically to the nature of what type of problem we're trying to solve.

Q: Are there any specific tools you encourage people to use when brainstorming?

PB: We tend to use a wide range of low-tech tools. Drawing and art plays a major role in brainstorming. We also use white boards, Post-It Notes, and even toys to facilitate the creative process. We're also very disciplined. If we're going to spend time brainstorming, we need to stay focused enough to develop solutions. This isn't about goofing off and having fun. We should always have something to show for our brainstorming efforts, even if it's determined that we don't yet have the right answer to a problem. To stay focused and on track, having someone work as the group facilitator is important. We set up the rules for the brainstorming session in advance and then make sure someone is there to record the ideas and keep people going in the right direction.

When things are slow from a creative standpoint, I'll sometimes have the group participate in a forced writing exercise. For example, I show a random photograph or picture of something and give people one minute to write something funny that relates to the picture and a birthday or anniversary. This forces people to document the first thought in their mind as opposed to over think it.

If I am working with photographers, I might develop an exercise that involves them shooting pictures around a specific theme. I tell them to go out and shoot only one roll of film, using a 33mm camera, in three hours, without using a flash. I have found that they'll often come back with a handful of pictures that are emotionally charged, breathtaking, and compelling, because they didn't have time to overthink anything and they shot their photographs from the heart.

I also find that teaming up two or more people who don't typically work together sometimes has very good results. It can be a bit awkward in the beginning, but once the people become comfortable with each other, they realize they each offer something unique to contribute toward finding the solution.

Q: **Do you encourage brainstorming alone or in groups?**

PB: We typically work in groups. I believe some of the best creative output will come from building ideas off each other and bouncing ideas around. Sometimes, working in a group will result in a small conflict or debate. It will be through the resolution of that debate that some really good ideas and solutions get generated. It's based on the theory that two, three, four, or five heads are better than one.

If everyone in the group is thinking and participating, what results is a truly collective effort, especially when you bring in people from diverse backgrounds or different problem-solving styles to work together.

Q: **What are some of the biggest challenges your teams face when trying to tap into creativity?**

PB: For us, we need to make sure that we don't over-systematize the creative process. We don't want to put constraints on the process either. There's a certain type of magic involved with brainstorming and creative thinking. I don't think we truly know where it comes from or control it. I think, however, we can direct it and focus it. Most musicians, artists and dancers, for example, learn how to focus their creative energies to produce something wonderful. This process often defies logic in terms of how it can be structured.

The challenge is being able to unleash people's creative abilities, but at the same time, maintaining discipline and focus, so we get done what needs to get done. This is a very fine line. We want people to be as creative as possible, but we also want the outcome to have value for our business and product lines.

Q: **What happens when the ideas don't flow? How do you deal with these situations?**

PB: This does happen. It's not necessarily something that can be controlled. When it happens, you need to move on to another problem, mix up the teams, or take a different approach to the brainstorming. Some people have the fear that one day, their creative well is going to dry up and they'll run out of ideas. In reality, this is never going to happen.

Sometimes, you can have a creative block as a result of something that happens in your personal life. September 11th is a perfect example. For some people on our staff, this was a tremendous source of inspiration. These people created beautiful poetry and artwork relating to the tragedy. For others, it served as a creative block, because they could not focus as a result of being so distracted by the disaster that took place.

Q: **When you're working on a highly creative project, how do you know when it's complete and refrain from over-thinking the final idea so it never gets finished?**

PB: Most of the time, if you start with a clear vision or purpose for what you're being creative about and what you're trying to accomplish, knowing when you're finished becomes pretty straight forward. Your desired outcome serves as a reality check and something to compare your ideas against.

One of the skills creative people have is being able to discern something that's average or mediocre against something that's truly good. The ability to say, "That's it!" or "Eureka!" is a skill most people naturally have, but it needs to be compared to the objective. It's all about keeping focus on the end objective and not going too far off track. Sometimes, it's the facilitator in the brainstorming session who we rely on to keep the creative people on track. Remember, creative problem solving is not linear. Sometimes, tangential thinking really pays off.

Q: **Once an idea is decided upon, what's your process for implementing it?**

PB: Once we have a clear idea of what we want to do as a result of a brainstorming or planning session, we then utilize our well-defined work processes that involve bringing the right people in on the project, such as the writer, artist, photographer, or sculptor, to help refine and execute the idea. Once the idea is properly executed, it goes to manufacturing and through distribution, etc. We utilize our experts to implement ideas. Creative people have much more to offer than just creativity. They have excellent cognitive skills as well, that should not be overlooked.

Q: **After you know what idea will be implemented, how do you sell the idea to the experts you bring in to execute it?**

PB: This is often done through a kickoff meeting. We'll bring the various experts who will implement the idea together with the creative team. The goal is to get everyone to emotionally buy into what we're trying to accomplish. When people are emotionally attached to a product, they'll invest their emotions into it, not just their skills. We try to avoid a basic hand off from one department to the next. Everyone involved in a project is made to feel valuable as part of the process and the team. If you can tap into the emotion and passion of everyone working on a large team, it really does show through in the final implementation.

Q: **What is a "blue sky" project at Hallmark?**

PB: These are long-term projects where we don't know what the exact strategy is or what the final outcome will be. We know that if you bring a talented group of people together and ask them a provocative question, they'll oftentimes amaze you. One example of this was a recent "blue sky" project.

Someone came up with the concept that one of the things people are most drawn to is light. Light captures people's attention. We wanted to combine emotion and feeling with light. We gathered a team together and asked, "If Hallmark were to combine emotion and light, what would that look like? How would light and emotions manifest themselves together?" We sent the team off to an innovation center to work for a period of time. We didn't know what they were going to do or what they'd come up with.

They came back with some of the most amazing concept and product ideas that we've ever seen. We would never have been able to conceive of these ideas unless we took the "blue sky" approach. Many of the ideas are now being developed into patented products because they are so different.

Q: **In your opinion, how do deadlines impact creativity?**

PB: Deadlines can be a good thing and a bad thing. They force us to be disciplined. Ultimately, during a brainstorming session, you have to stop developing ideas and then focus on one to create a solution. A deadline can be good for that. If a deadline is unrealistic, however, we could find ourselves compromising solutions, because we're trying to get something out too fast. The people who set the deadlines need to be very careful. You want to keep things moving and keep people focused, but you don't want to compromise the end result.

Q: **For someone who is first learning how to tap into their creativity, what advice do you have for them?**

PB: Give yourself permission to be creative! There are so many influences in our lives that tell us not to think creatively because we have to conform to the norm. We're taught we have to act a certain way. That's wrong. If you were to give an adult a crayon and ask him or her to draw a giraffe, most people would create a drawing at the level of a 12-year-old. In other words, if you were to compare the adult's drawing to that of a 12-year-old, they'd be at the same skill level.

This is attributable to the fact that between the ages of 10 and 12, most of us have our crayons taken away. We're told, "Drawing with crayons is for little kids. Big boys and girls don't do that."

Sometimes, you'll see adults doodle during meetings or when they're on the phone. This is simply an urge they have to be creative and somehow express that creativity. When you're doodling, your mind is doing some amazing things. It's that creative problem solving process that we tend to shut down consciously or subconsciously.

For someone first learning to be creative, they need to give themselves permission to tap into their creativity. It's okay to stare at the sky, doodle, daydream, keep a journal, play a musical instrument, and to somehow find a creative voice. If you don't give yourself permission, you will never find your creative voice.

I think taking risks is also part of being a creative thinker. Some of the best creative talents are also some of the most disciplined. What they do may look like a haphazard process from the outside, but they are highly disciplined in their problem solving process. Being creative is hard work. It can, however, be one of the most personally rewarding experiences you'll ever have.

If you don't know how to get started, go out and buy some crayons, clay, Silly Putty, or Legos, for example, and start playing in a creative way. When you're playing with clay and using your motor skills, your mind is creatively solving problems. This is a great way to tap into a part of your brain that you might not normally tap into.

All of us have creative problem-solving abilities. Some of us are just better at using them than others, because we practice. We have the ability, the skill, or a talent that allows us to tap into our creativity.

Q: Is it possible to make a mistake when brainstorming?

PB: Absolutely! Sometimes, we shut ourselves down because we become too judgmental of our own ideas or someone else's ideas. People also become too self-critical or possessive. If you think your idea is better than everyone else's, you won't be open to listening to other people's ideas or points of view. That's a big mistake!

Carol Dubron-Witlin and Peggy Filis-Burkhardt

Title: Cofounders

Company: OWN THE POWER

Website: *www.OWNTHEPOWER.com*

Background

Some brainstorming sessions result in ideas capable of helping others survive the trials and tribulations of life. Others generate ideas around which successful businesses are created and built. When Carol and Peggy embarked on a brainstorming session together, they created a business idea that would ultimately inspire countless other people, and it's all based around the inspirational slogan, "OWN THE POWER."

Before launching OWN THE POWER, Carol worked as an elementary school teacher, a marriage and family therapist, and later returned to school and earned a law degree. She then worked for several years in civil litigation and estate planning.

While involved in a charity project, Carol was introduced to her current friend and business partner, Peggy. Prior to OWN THE POWER, Peggy had a successful career in television marketing, working for stations in New York, Washington, D.C., and Boston. When her father suddenly died in 1982, Peggy took over her family's food marketing business, which she later sold. After that, she worked for a dot-com business which she cofounded.

Once the two realized they shared the same core philosophies about achieving success through determination, passion, and creativity, they decided to become business partners. The next step was to brainstorm and generate a business idea. In 2001, OWN THE POWER was born.

OWN THE POWER's primary goal is to help people tap into their reservoir of personal power and fulfill their dreams. The OWN THE POWER product line was created to help people break free of negative thoughts and behaviors by harnessing the power of focus.

The product line was created to assist people in their journey to break free of negative behavior and gain control of their lives. This is accomplished by tapping into their deep reserve of personal strength and unlimited potential. Each product serves as a tangible sign of someone's innate power to create the life they want, plus remind them of their inner strength and potential.

OWN THE POWER bracelets and jewelry products, for example, help people focus on their personal commitment to achieving their dreams.

Concentrating on goals will make people's desire grow stronger. That increased desire will help transform mere thoughts into action that generates results.

Wearing an OWN THE POWER bracelet, for example, won't automatically make you a creative thinker, but it can be used as a motivational and inspirational tool for helping you implement your ideas and make them a reality. This has been proven many times by people who wear OWN THE POWER bracelets, including all of the top 30 finalists on Fox Television's *American Idol* series.

OWN THE POWER bracelets

After receiving the bracelets as a gift from recording artist/judge Paula Abdul, the contestants spontaneously talked about the benefits they achieved from their OWN THE POWER bracelets when they were interviewed on shows like *Entertainment Tonight* and for newspaper articles that appeared in places like *USA Today*. These were unpaid and unsolicited testimonials.

(Some information within the previous section is from press material provided courtesy of the associated individual or company.)

Interview With Carol Dubron-Witlin and Peggy Filis-Burkhardt

Q: **How did the concept for OWN THE POWER as well as the slogan come about?**

PF: It was through a brainstorming session. We came up with many viable business ideas, but we didn't have the passion to pursue them. When we came up with the basic concept for OWN THE POWER, we had that "ah-ha" moment and realized we were onto something. We're trying to communicate and teach a philosophy with our products, not just start a trend of the moment.

CD: The OWN THE POWER bracelets and jewelry are an outgrowth of the underling concept behind the company. It's about taking initiative and doing things for yourself. Our intention wasn't to get into the jewelry business. Jewelry was the most tactile, tangible representation of the OWN THE POWER concept.

Q: **What's the purpose of the OWN THE POWER bracelets?**

PF: We hope to help people change their consciousness by becoming aware of their own power. We want people to think about their own power as many times per day as they possibly can. It's only possible to hold one conscious thought in your mind at any given time. We want people to associate their OWN THE POWER bracelet with a positive thought, and then think about that positive thought every time the see or feel the bracelet on their wrist. We want people to say, "I own the power to_____" then fill in the blank for themselves. That's the thought we hope will keep popping up in their consciousness as a result of wearing the bracelet or other piece of OWN THE POWER jewelry. We are what we think.

CD: Anyone can go to a self-help seminar or read a self-help book. Once the experience of seeing the seminar or reading the book is over, that experience is gone from your life. The OWN THE POWER jewelry serves as a constant reminder for whatever it is you want to own the power to do. On the bracelets and charms, for example, the words "OWN THE POWER" are raised, so they can be seen and touched.

Q: **Prior to starting OWN THE POWER, had either of you had successful experiences with brainstorming?**

PF: When I cofounded the dot-com company, we spend the first three months of our existence overanalyzing everything. We thought that it was important to have all of the answers before we actually started doing business. This was an analytical way of thinking, which turned out to be wrong. We soon discovered that we'd never have *all* of the answers. The marketplace is always changing. Doing research and homework is important, but so is taking that creative step and being open to new possibilities and opportunities. I have always utilized brainstorming in my work. My core business philosophy is that there are no rules and that you need to throw up all of the ideas and eliminate the bad ones later.

CD: For me, brainstorming is a relatively new concept. But, it's one we've used successfully many times in the creation and operation of OWN THE POWER.

Q: **These days, do you consciously plan brainstorming sessions for the ongoing operation of your business?**

PF: It's just the two of us, so our approach is very casual. A brainstorming session could kick off as a result of a conversation. We are both avid readers. What we read often impacts what we talk about. It also inspires many of our ideas. One of our latest projects evolved around our charity work and our wish to help breast cancer survivors. We're currently brainstorming ideas for a product designed to inspire people with breast cancer.

CD: We should make it clear that we have absolutely no experience in the jewelry business. Once we decided that our message would be conveyed best through jewelry products, we needed to learn all about the jewelry manufacturing and sales business. We had to overcome our fear of asking questions in order to obtain the knowledge we needed.

Q: **During and after you brainstorm, how do you evaluate your ideas?**

PF: We just know when we have an idea that is good. Carol and I are very different people. When we both agree an idea is good, that's usually an indication to move forward. If one of us is passionate about an idea, but the other person doesn't have strong objections, we might also move forward. All other ideas get dropped. It's all about finding that 'ah-ha' moment.

CD: We've also used brainstorming to develop potential new markets for our bracelets. For example, we sell our OWN THE POWER bracelets through our Website, but also through specialty gift stores and day spas, for example. We're also developing relationships with various charity organizations. We always take our ideas out into the marketplace and bounce them off other people.

Q: **Once an idea is generated, what process do you use to implement your ideas?**

PF: We figure out everything that needs to be done to implement the idea. For example, once we decided to pursue the jewelry idea, we needed to start working with jewelry designers. We then had to communicate our vision to them. What we wanted to create was not a traditional jewelry product. We met with at least six designers before making any decisions, because it was difficult finding people who had the same vision we had for our ideas. We then had to learn all about the jewelry manufacturing business. Our bracelets have a rubber component to them. I can't tell you how much research we did about rubber. Usually, there are no easy answers when it comes to implementing an idea.

CD: As we moved forward, we never relinquished any core business responsibilities to anyone else. We worked with the experts and specialists we needed to, but we did a lot of learning on our own. In this business, we both wear dozens of hats in terms of the responsibilities we take on.

Q: How can people use your bracelets or other jewelry to help them achieve their goals?

PF: I don't know if wearing a bracelet can make you more creative. What it can do is help you focus more on your objectives and goals, especially when it comes to implementing your ideas. In *USA Today,* when asked why Paula Abdul gave the OWN THE POWER bracelets to the 30 finalists of *American Idol,* is quoted as saying, "These contestants are going through the most rigorous challenge week-to-week, having to rise above adversity. They're being crushed by the nasty Brit [judge Simon Cowell] and some are breaking down. I could not handle seeing that. It clicked that this would be such the perfect reminder to believe in themselves."

Robert Schwartz

Title:	Executive Creative Director
Company:	TBWA\Chiat-Day Advertising
Website:	*www.tbwa.com*

TBWA\CHIAT\DAY

Robert Schwartz, Executive Creative Director of TBWA\Chiat-Day

Background

TBWA\Chiat-Day is a leading global marketing and corporate communications company operating in more than 100 countries. It currently works with more than 5,000 clients, including Apple Computer, Adidas, Energizer, Infiniti, Mars (makers of M&Ms, TWIX and Snickers candy), Nissan, and Sony PlayStation. With almost 9,000 employees spread throughout 214 offices, TBWA is one of the most prestigious and powerful advertising agencies in the world.

Robert Schwartz is the Executive Creative Director at TBWA\Chiat-Day. From the company's Los Angeles office, he personally works with multiple accounts, including Nissan.

Virtually all of Robert's work involves creativity and brainstorming on behalf of his clients. In this interview, he shares some of his personal advice on what it takes for anyone to become an expert brainstormer and creative thinker.

(Some information within the previous section is from press material provided courtesy of the associated individual or company.)

Interview With Robert Schwartz

Q: **How did you get into advertising?**

RS: I fell into it. I graduated from The University of Michigan, but didn't know what I wanted to do with my life. I decided to participate in the Outward Bound program, which is designed to teach people that they can achieve anything. I then had a couple boring jobs in publishing. A woman I worked with back then suggested that I might enjoy working in advertising. She suggested I take a class in advertising. So, I began attending The School of Visual Arts at night.

I ultimately landed a job in advertising as a proofreader. At one point, the company I was working with became too busy, so they asked if I'd be interested in working on some accounts. That's how I got started.

Q: **When did you discover that you were extremely creative?**

RS: I don't think there was a point I ever made that discovery. I just knew early on that I could not do math. For me, I chose advertising through a process of elimination. As I began taking classes, I was taught what good advertising and communication was, but I don't recall ever taking any classes that specifically taught me how to be creative. I know some people who work in advertising have taken improvisational acting classes to enhance their creativity.

Q: **Having worked on advertising campaigns for many major accounts, what keeps you inspired?**

RS: First, I need to be able to afford the tuition for my kids' private school. For me, I enjoy working with companies that have large budgets and that have the ability to inject positive messages into the world. Companies with multimillion-dollar ad budgets can communicate positive or negative messages. I want the work I do to be positive. For this reason, I have personally turned down work from potential clients. I was approached to work for a cigarette company, for example, but I chose not to pursue it.

Q: **When you start working with a new client, where do the ideas for the company's advertising campaign come from?**

RS: One thing I have learned over the years is that good ideas can come from anywhere. A lot of agencies are structured where only the creative department is allowed to come up with and implement ideas. The way we are set up is that we accept good ideas from anywhere. We have an open door, open mind, and open ear policy when it comes to generating new ideas. We encourage input from everyone within the organization, even if they're not working on a specific account. We also take ideas directly from our clients. Our clients know all about their own products and/or services, so we take their expert input as well.

Q: **How does a typical brainstorming session work when you're involved?**

RS: There are many ways to brainstorm. I believe when you have a brainstorming session, one of the first things you need to do is set up the rules of engagement. This could be as simple as telling the people involved that the session they're about to participate in is all about diarrhea of the mouth, that there are no boundaries. It's about anything goes. The brainstorming session is not the edit session. By its very nature, it should generate a bunch of ideas that are good, bad, sublime, and ridiculous. It's about giving people the freedom to throw ideas up on the wall and allow everything to stick. That's the key to kicking off a great session.

After the ideas are generated, they need to be properly analyzed and implemented, or else all you did was an exercise[...]that didn't ultimately solve anything.

Q: **Do you use any special brainstorming techniques?**

RS: At TBWA, one exercise we participate in on an agency-wide basis is called "disruption." This is a methodology for thinking. You start off with the convention of something, which is the commonly accepted way of thinking. What you want to do is disrupt those conventions to lead to a vision. For Nissan, for example, it wanted to be known as the boldest, most thoughtful car company on the planet. All car companies just show off and sell cars. We're disrupting that conventional way of thinking through the advertising by selling the idea of change.

Another exercise we encourage is for people to do a 180. We spend time thinking about everything that is totally inappropriate for a new product, for example. If we're working with a shiny new product that people would expect to see in a beautiful product shot within an advertisement, we'll consider shooting that product in a pile of mud. It's 180 degrees from what you'd expect to see. This concept helps us generate new ideas. For example, the fresh and clean new product might emerge from the mud in the commercial. Sometimes, when you think about inappropriateness, there's always a kernel of appropriateness within the idea.

Q: When you brainstorm, do you always start with a specific goal or objective?

RS: You're typically better off doing that. If you just brainstorm for the sake of it, you'll always find yourself caught in the storm. The purpose of a brainstorm is to lead you to a dryer place, metaphorically speaking. The sun always shines at the end of the storm.

Q: Do you typically brainstorm alone or in a group?

RS: Both. When I am planning to brainstorm with a group, I always give out a homework assignment in advance. I require the people who will be involved to spend some time thinking about the topic before the brainstorming session. This way, they come into the session with some preliminary ideas, which is our starting point. It's very hard for people to just step into a room and generate incredible ideas on the spot if they haven't done advanced preparation.

Q: What is the perfect environment for you to brainstorm in?

RS: I tend to work better off-site. Wherever you typically work, I suggest leaving that place and going somewhere else. If you're very familiar with an environment, you're more apt to be distracted by everyday things. Also, if you are inhibited in your office, you might find you're more uninhibited away from the office. The little shift of geography tends to help liberate the mind.

Q: Is there a way to create a good brainstorming environment in any office situation?

RS: Sure there is. I think you always need a marker and a large pad to write everything down. I also think you always need some kind of food on hand. I always recommend M&Ms, since Mars, Inc. is one of my clients. The sugar rush will help get people's brain going. Eating also takes people's minds away from the main purpose of the session, so their brain can quickly recharge. I've never thought about how lighting or the formation of the furniture impacts a brainstorming session.

Based on what I have discovered, people tend to work better if they're not overly relaxed. Shorter meetings occur when people have to stand. Longer meetings happen when people are comfortably seated and relaxed. To brainstorm, somewhere in the middle of these two extremes is probably the best environment.

Q: **Aside from a marker and a large pad, do you utilize any other brainstorming tools during a typical session?**

RS: It all depends. When we meet with a client, for example, we're usually bringing together people who think very linearly. It's always good to preplan some kind of exercise that will get these people out of their logical thinking mode. For example, we'll hand people a potato and a straw and tell each of them to get the straw cleanly through the potato. By the very nature of the exercise, we're putting people into a more creative and playful state of mind. The goal is for them to figure something out. The solution is actually very simple, but many brilliant people can't figure it out too quickly.

After participating in a fun and challenging activity, people are more open to new ideas and to thinking in new directions. I believe that during a brainstorming session, it's perfectly okay to make work time into play time.

Q: **When people think of advertising executives generating ideas, they often associate that process with the creation of storyboards. Is this actually the case?**

RS: Not usually. Storyboards are used for communicating the ideas for a story or a commercial, for example, after the ideas have already been created. Using those ideas, an artist comes in and creates a colorful storyboard that communicates the script and visuals for an ad. Sometimes, when we're kicking around ideas that translate into a story, I will quickly sketch out six boxes on a sheet of paper, for example, and fill in those boxes with words or rough pencil sketches.

Q: **How do you work creatively when you're forced to work under tight deadlines or excessive pressure?**

RS: Good planning is what's required in these situations. I personally either get something in the first five minutes or the last five minutes. You can give me two weeks to work on something, but the ideas will either come right away or at the last minute. What's great about deadlines is that there's an unmistakable endpoint to the thinking. How you work with deadlines all depends on the type of person you are.

Some people like to do a little bit of work every single day leading up to a deadline. Others like to leave things for the last second and work really well under pressure. It really helps to know what type of person you are and understand what the task is at hand.

Q: **Have you discovered any ways of making pressure work in your favor when you're being creative?**

RS: Often times I'll be close to a deadline and I'll see some work and know it's not right. Sometimes, with the rejection of the initial idea and the knowledge that the clock is ticking, it spurs a new or better idea or approach.

Q: **After a brainstorming session, what process do you use to evaluate your ideas and choose the best ones?**

RS: What we like to do is have each of the participants vote on the ideas after the session. In between the brainstorming session and the voting, however, we'll always take a break for at least 45 minutes. When everyone comes back into the room, their minds are clear and we vote on each idea.

After the vote, we wait several hours or even a few days. We then revisit those ideas which were popular in the vote and evaluate them again. We'll also take our list of good ideas and show them to someone who wasn't involved at all in the brainstorming session. This gives us additional feedback.

Q: **Once you decide on the idea with which you plan to move forward, how do you create a plan for implementation?**

RS: When you have something that you want to go with, the main thing that needs to be done in order to make it successful is to commit 100 percent to the idea. Everyone has to get rallied around the idea. It's almost like creating a blood pact to insure success. After that, I think people should divide up into teams and take on different responsibilities that relate to the implementation. Everyone is a specialist in something and their unique abilities need to be exploited during the idea implementation process.

Q: **What is the biggest challenge you face when tapping your creativity and implementing your ideas?**

RS: The biggest challenge is making the commitment to do something. Part of it is just getting off your butt and overcoming laziness and insecurity.

Q: **When you're implementing an idea or even developing ideas, how do you know when the task is complete?**

RS: That's like asking "When does a poet know when the poem is finished?" To be honest, I am disgustingly pragmatic. The task is finished when you're out of time. This philosophy works.

Q: **For someone who is first learning how to tap into their creativity, what advice can you offer?**

RS: First, you need to believe that everyone is creative. This includes people who have analytical jobs working all day with spreadsheets. Next, the best thing someone can do is start generating stuff that's creative. It doesn't matter what you do, but creative thinking isn't real until you make it real.

Q: **What do you think holds most people back from successfully brainstorming?**

RS: I think the biggest thing that holds people back is their personal insecurities. Most of our schooling does not encourage creativity. We're taught to stay in line, follow directions, and think logically. Part of thinking creatively is looking at the status quo on anything and thinking of ways you can do it better or differently.

To be creative, you can't just live at your office, work on your computer, and stew in your own thoughts. You have to communicate with other people. Ideas, both good and bad, are meant to be shared. When you share ideas, cool things happen. People will think your ideas are great and help you execute them, or they'll say something like, "That idea isn't exactly right. What if you did this?" With other people, you can start playing the "what if" game and move thoughts into entirely different areas.

Final Thoughts

Hopefully, this book has helped you not only to learn how to be more creative, but also to discover the importance of being a creative thinker in your personal, professional, and financial life. Reading this book is just the beginning. You now need to begin practicing by utilizing what you've learned. Start applying it to the problems you encounter and the opportunities you seek out.

Hallmark's Paul Barker stated, "From a business perspective, business leaders need to be open and trusting to the creative process, even if it might look odd. If you think about what challenges business are going to be faced with in the not so distant future, it's clear that the easy solutions have already been arrived at. That means that what's left are the tough solutions to face the tough challenges that lie ahead. I think to solve those problems through creativity and ingenuity, rather than by other means, is probably going to be the best approach to take."

Business leaders need to encourage their workforce to be more creative in order to solve problems. New ideas, passion, and creative energies need to be tapped into as a business resource. It is creative thinking that will allow companies to grow their businesses and prosper.

"We need to teach our children to be more creative in school. We need to enable the creative thinking process, not work to shut it down," added Barker. "Even in world government, we need to think creatively to find solutions to global problems and disagreements."

Creative thinking and problem-solving can truly impact every aspect of our lives, and brainstorming can be the catalyst to generate those awesome ideas that lead to the tremendous results we all want and need.

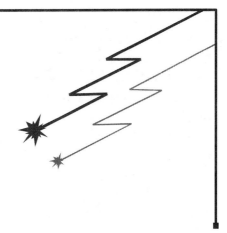

Index

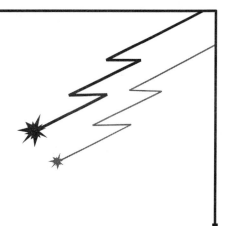

About the Author

Jason R. Rich (*www.JasonRich.com*) is the author of more than 25 books on a wide range of topics. He's also an accomplished newspaper and magazine columnist, as well as a marketing, PR, and creativity consultant to businesses. He lives just outside of Boston.